CONTENTS

NATHANIEL
WOLFE
AND THE BODYSNATCHERS

NATHANIEL WOLFE

AND THE BODYSNATCHERS

BRIAN KEANEY

ORCHARD BOOKS

ORCHARD BOOKS
338 Euston Road, London NW1 3BH
Orchard Books Australia
Level 17/207 Kent Street, Sydney, NSW 2000

First published in 2009 by Orchard Books
A paperback original

ISBN 978 1 84616 574 0

A CIP catalogue record for this book is available from the British Library.

1 3 5 7 9 10 8 6 4 2

Printed in Great Britain

Orchard Books is a division of Hachette Children's Books,
an Hachette UK company.
www.hachette.co.uk

1. LIGHTS IN THE GRAVEYARD

Lady Huntercombe was a thin woman with a pointed nose and a rather distrustful expression. She peered across the dining table at Nathaniel until he felt like a specimen in a glass jar. 'So you are the famous Ghost Hunter of London?' she remarked.

Nathaniel thought carefully before replying to this. On their walk to the house earlier that evening, his grandfather had explained that Lady Huntercombe was the real head of the household. 'Her husband goes along with whatever she says. And she has a great deal of influence in high places. So watch what you say to her.'

'Well, that's what the newspapers called me,' Nathaniel admitted. 'I didn't choose the name myself.'

'But it's true that you foiled the plans of that dreadful man, Mr Chesterfield, who had killed his wife and wanted to kill his stepdaughter? And that you did so after seeing an apparition of some kind?'

'Yes, that's true,' Nathaniel agreed.

'How extraordinary!'

No more extraordinary than this dinner party, Nathaniel felt like telling her. Four people at a table big enough to seat twenty with ease! Enough dishes for half a dozen meals! A whole tribe of servants bowing and scraping for all they were worth! It simply didn't make sense. Yet for twelve months now, this had been his life – kitted out like a gentleman in the finest clothes, rubbing shoulders with the wealthiest people in the county. Bored to death.

How he longed for the days when he had lived in the slums of the East End of London, trying to keep out of the landlady's sight because there was no money to pay the rent, carrying trays of fish around Billingsgate Market all day in order to earn the price of a meat pie. He missed the sights and sounds, and even the smells of the city. 'You'll love the peace and quiet of the countryside,' his friends had told him when he first announced that he was moving out of London to live with his grandfather, and he had smiled back and assured them that he was looking forward to it. But you could have too much peace and quiet, and Nathaniel was beginning to feel about a hundred years old. You can take the boy out of the gutter, he said to himself, but can you ever take the gutter out of the boy?

Lady Huntercombe turned to Nathaniel's grandfather. 'Mr Monkton, you should have brought your grandson to see us before. You mustn't let him hide his light under a bushel. We are all so excited to hear about his adventures. Aren't we, dear?' She addressed this last remark to her husband.

'What was that?' Lord Huntercombe was a red-faced man with enormous side-whiskers and a nose so mottled and blotched from years of drinking fine wines it looked like something that had been left under the sea and colonised by barnacles. He had at least two spare chins and his waistcoat buttons strained against the substantial bulge of his belly. He rested his clasped hands on that bulge like a man in prayer, while he considered whether or not he could manage the enormous slice of cake being offered by one of his servants.

'I said, we are most keen to hear about Nathaniel's exploits,' Lady Huntercombe repeated.

'Oh yes, quite so,' Lord Huntercombe agreed, reluctantly turning down the cake and settling for another glass of wine instead.

'There's really not much to tell you,' Nathaniel said. 'Mr Chesterfield was planning to murder his stepdaughter, Sophie. And he probably would have succeeded, but the ghost of his wife appeared to me one night, and from then on she refused to leave me in peace until I managed to stop him. With a lot of help from my friends, of course.'

'But you actually saw the ghost?'

'Yes.'

To himself, Nathaniel thought, She would like to keep me here as her pet, to entertain her with stories of the supernatural, to show off to her friends. But he was nobody's pet, and though she continued to quiz him about the details of his adventure, his answers grew less and less informative until she was forced to abandon the subject altogether.

'That business in Harford Cemetery last week was a most shocking affair,' Lord Huntercombe remarked. Apart from eating and drinking, His Lordship's interests were largely confined to shooting small animals. So whatever had happened in Harford Cemetery the previous week must have been very unusual indeed to have attracted his attention. Nathaniel pricked up his ears.

'A very bad business,' his wife agreed. 'What I want to know is what you're going to do about it, Mr Monkton?'

'What *I'm* going to do about it?' Nathaniel's grandfather replied.

'Well, you *are* the magistrate for the area, after all.'

Mr Monkton sighed. 'That is true, madam,' he conceded, 'but though I can sentence the villains when they are caught, there is very little that is within my power until that time.'

Lady Huntercombe shook her head. 'It is not good enough, Mr Monkton, not good enough at all. These villains must be put behind bars right away!'

'What is everyone talking about?' Nathaniel asked.

'Bodysnatchers!' Lord Huntercombe informed him.

Nathaniel turned to his grandfather for an explanation.

'Last Wednesday, a man called Robert Pearce was buried in Harford Cemetery,' his grandfather told him. 'That same night, someone dug up his grave and stole his body.'

'The same thing happened last month across the border in Hampshire,' Lady Huntercombe chipped in. 'On that occasion two bodies were taken. I don't know what the world is coming to.'

'But why would anyone want to steal a body?' Nathaniel asked.

'So that unscrupulous medical men can cut them up,' his grandfather replied.

When Nathaniel continued to look blank, his grandfather explained, 'There have been many advances in medicine in recent years, and those advances have come about because people have learned more about the human body. Much of that knowledge has come from the examination of dead bodies.'

'Isn't that a good thing?' Nathaniel asked.

'Most certainly. But because of the demand to know still more, a trade has sprung up in cadavers, and that is certainly not a good thing.'

'So people are digging up corpses to sell them?' Nathaniel said.

'Exactly.'

'That's terrible.'

'It's monstrous,' Lady Huntercombe agreed. 'The distress caused to the families of the victims is indescribable. In my opinion, the army should be posted around our cemeteries.'

'I think that might be taking things a little too far,' Mr Monkton suggested. 'I have no doubt that those responsible will be apprehended in due course.'

Lady Huntercombe looked far from satisfied with this reply, but her husband soon began to tire of the subject and started to talk about a new horse he was thinking of buying.

Eventually, the meal was consumed and the company withdrew to the drawing room. Nathaniel glanced behind him as he left. The table was still laden with half-eaten food: a huge bowl of trifle, several different varieties of cake, fresh fruit, jugs of cream. He could easily imagine how much work had been involved in preparing the meal and how much would still have to be done before the servants could retire for the night. But he suspected that this was something to which Lord and Lady Huntercombe never gave the slightest thought. His Lordship cares more about the welfare of his horses and his hounds than he does about his servants, Nathaniel thought to himself. But that was how it was with the upper classes – or with most of them, anyway. They never thought about the lower orders unless they were absolutely forced to.

When the clock struck eleven, Mr Monkton decided that it was time to return home. Nathaniel, who had been trying hard to stifle a yawn for the last five minutes, willingly agreed.

'You must come and see us again,' Lady Huntercombe said, fixing her eyes on Nathaniel as he put on his coat.

Nathaniel did his best to smile back at her. But he thought to himself, not if I can help it!

'I'll just ring and tell the footman to bring the carriage round to the front entrance,' Lord Huntercombe announced.

Mr Monkton shook his head. 'Thank you for the offer, sir, but we came on foot and we will return in the same way. It is less than a mile to the village and the moon is full. The exercise will be good for us. What do you say, Nathaniel?'

Nathaniel nodded eagerly. After several hours of sitting around, making polite conversation with the Huntercombes, a moonlit walk through country lanes was just what he needed.

A few minutes later he and his grandfather had said farewell to their hosts and were breathing in the cool night air as they made their way towards the village where their house was situated.

Though he was in his sixties, Mr Monkton was a fit man, and the two of them walked briskly along in companionable silence. Above them, ragged clouds raced across the sky, hiding the moon from time to time and plunging the world into pitch darkness. The sheer emptiness and quiet of the countryside, especially at night-time, was one of the things Nathaniel had found hardest to get used to since leaving the city. Even in the small hours, the streets of London were awash with drunken revellers, homeless beggars, ruthless criminals or just ordinary citizens who could not sleep. But out here in the country, the night belonged to the wild creatures, and mankind seemed to be trespassing. It made him distinctly uneasy.

As they came within sight of the village, Nathaniel suddenly noticed lights moving about in the graveyard.

Stopping in his tracks, he seized his grandfather's arm and pointed them out.

'Do you think it could be bodysnatchers?' he whispered.

'I don't know,' Mr Monkton replied, 'but if it is, I'll soon put a stop to them.' He immediately set off in the direction of the churchyard gate.

'It might be best to creep up, unnoticed,' Nathaniel suggested, hurrying alongside him.

But Mr Monkton was in no mood for caution. 'Lady Huntercombe was right. I do represent the law in this part of the country,' he told his grandson, 'and if there's wrong-doing of any kind, then it's my job to see that it's dealt with.'

That was all very well, Nathaniel thought to himself, but Lady Huntercombe didn't have to confront criminals in a midnight graveyard.

Mr Monkton opened the churchyard gate, stepped inside and called out in a loud voice, 'You there! What do you think you're doing?'

There was no sound except the distant hoot of an owl.

The moon chose that precise moment to go behind a cloud, and it was difficult to make out anything but the vague shapes of the tombstones. Nevertheless, it was clear that the light was coming from the far corner of the churchyard, the area where the newer graves were dug. 'We'd better go and investigate more closely!' Mr Monkton declared.

They made their way uncertainly along the little path that wove erratically through the graves. Twice Nathaniel stumbled on the uneven ground and barked his shins against unseen objects. Then suddenly, the moon emerged from behind the clouds and the churchyard was illuminated almost as brightly as by day. Three men were standing beside a newly dug pile of earth. Two of them were intent on hauling up a coffin with ropes while the third held a lantern over the grave.

'Stop that this instant!' Mr Monkton ordered.

The three men turned and looked at him. The one who was holding the lantern put it down on the ground. Calmly, and without taking his eyes off Mr Monkton for one moment, he reached into his pocket and brought out a pistol.

'I suggest you go home and mind your own business, old man,' he said, cocking the pistol and pointing it directly at Nathaniel's grandfather.

'This *is* my business,' Mr Monkton declared. 'I am the magistrate for this area.'

'Then it ain't your lucky day,' replied the bodysnatcher.

After that, everything happened in slow-motion. The bodysnatcher's finger squeezed the trigger of the pistol. There was a noise that seemed as loud as thunder to Nathaniel and a simultaneous flash of gunpowder. Then his grandfather crumpled to the ground, clutching his chest.

'Grandad!' Nathaniel cried out, bending over his grandfather, hoping desperately that the old man was still alive.

His grandfather moaned.

Just then Nathaniel felt a shadow fall over him. Looking up, he saw that the bodysnatcher was standing directly above him and the pistol was raised once more.

Nathaniel froze. So this is how I die, he thought to himself, for there was no mercy in the bodysnatcher's eyes. The man's face was gaunt and ugly, the skin pitted and scarred. One of his ears was terribly mutilated, as if it had been torn off by a wild animal. He seemed like the inhabitant of some other, more terrible world, a place without joy or pity, where a human being was no more than a walking carcass, to be cut down and sold to the highest bidder.

'Say your prayers, boy,' the bodysnatcher said. His finger tightened on the trigger once more and Nathaniel wondered, briefly, if it would hurt very much when the bullet entered his body.

With a click, the hammer struck the firing pin, but there was no explosion. The gunpowder had failed to ignite. Cursing, the man strode rapidly away and the two others followed at his heels.

Only when they had gone did Nathaniel find that he could move again. He felt almost dizzy with relief.

'Grandad, are you all right?' he asked. But his grandfather made no reply. Nathaniel put out his hand to touch the old man and found that his jacket was soaked with blood. It was clear that he was gravely wounded.

Horrified, Nathaniel leapt to his feet. 'Don't die, Grandad,' he said. 'I'm going to get help. I'll be back as quickly as I can. Just please don't die!'

He set off for his grandfather's house, running as fast as he could. As he ran, he blamed himself for what had happened. He had been the one to point the lights out to his grandfather. 'Why did I open my mouth?' he asked himself. 'I should never have let him go in there. I should have insisted that we went back to the house and got some help.'

But it was too late for all that now. His grandfather's life was ebbing away in the cold, dark churchyard. He might even be dead already. The man who had offered him a chance to make something of his life! The man who had taken him in when his own father had abandoned him! He gave me everything and all I did was complain, Nathaniel told himself.

At last he reached the house and hammered repeatedly with the door-knocker. After what seemed like an age, James, the butler, opened the door. He stared at Nathaniel's dishevelled figure in astonishment

'Come quickly!' Nathaniel panted. 'Mr Monkton has been shot!'

2. THE HAUNTED CLERK

James was an elderly man and he had been fast asleep when Nathaniel's knocking had awoken him. But once he had grasped the fact that his master was lying in the churchyard possibly bleeding to death, he moved decisively. The footman was dispatched with the carriage to fetch the local doctor while a stretcher was improvised from two poles and a blanket. Then James and Nathaniel returned hastily to the graveyard.

To Nathaniel's great relief, his grandfather was still conscious, though he was too weak to talk. Somehow, between them, they got him onto the stretcher. Then they struggled through the graveyard and back to the house, lowering his grandfather onto a couch in the drawing room.

Mrs McQuade, the cook, was waiting with hot water and bandages. She was normally a very talkative woman. But on this occasion she was grim-faced and tight-lipped as she set about the job of bandaging her master's wound.

Nathaniel remained by his grandfather's side, feeling utterly helpless, until the doctor finally arrived and sent him out of the room. Going to bed was out of the question so he sat in the library and waited restlessly while the lonely hours ticked by. At last the library door opened and the doctor stepped inside.

Nathaniel sprang to his feet. 'How is he?' he demanded.

'That remains to be seen,' the doctor replied, gravely. 'However, he has been fortunate in this respect. The bullet struck him underneath his right shoulder and passed straight through his body, emerging just below his armpit. It has done considerable damage to the muscles, of course, but not, as far as I can tell, to any of his organs.'

'Then he's not going to die?'

'Well, he's lost a lot of blood and he's very weak. There is still the problem of infection. He's not a young man, remember. So we are not out of the woods yet, by any means. But he's asleep now and appears to be comfortable. I've done all I can for the time being and I'll be back in the morning to look in on him. If I were you, I should get some rest.'

With that, the doctor took his leave. Nathaniel went to have a look at his grandfather and found that James had already brought a mattress and bedding into the drawing room and was determined to spend the night beside his master. Nathaniel looked at the two old men and smiled. Though they were master and servant, they had been more like companions for many years. His grandfather was safe enough in the care of James. So Nathaniel said goodnight and retired to his bedroom. Now the weariness that he had kept at bay for so long descended upon him fully. He undressed as quickly as he could, climbed beneath the covers and closed his eyes. A moment later he was sound asleep.

It seemed only minutes later that he was woken, though he realised by the light streaming through a gap in the curtains that the morning must be well advanced. James was standing beside the bed.

'I'm sorry to disturb you, sir,' he said.

'My grandfather…' Nathaniel began, starting to spring out of bed.

James put out his hands to restrain him. 'Calm yourself, sir. Your grandfather is tolerably well this morning. He has eaten some toast and drunk a cup of tea. There is no need for concern on his behalf. Indeed, I was intending to let you sleep. Only a gentleman has called to see you.'

‘A gentleman?’

‘Yes, sir. By the name of Simeon Makepeace.’

‘But I don’t know anyone of that name.’

‘He asked for you specifically.’

Nathaniel sighed. ‘Very well. I’ll be down as soon as I’m dressed.’

It was probably something to do with his grandfather, he decided, as he put on his clothes. After all, he himself knew hardly anyone in the village, and it was not likely that one of his old friends would have made the journey from London without letting him know in advance.

When he entered the front parlour a few minutes later, he found his visitor waiting for him. Mr Simeon Makepeace turned out to be a thin man of about forty. His mouse-brown hair was thinning and he peered out at the world through a pair of glasses with lenses as thick as the bottom of a beer bottle. He was respectably dressed, though Nathaniel could not help noticing that the cuffs of his jacket were frayed and his fingers were stained with ink.

Nathaniel’s experience of both sides of life had given him a keen eye for a person’s social position. Mr Simeon Makepeace, he concluded, was obviously in regular employment but not highly paid. At a guess, Nathaniel would have said he was a clerk of some kind. Perhaps he had been involved in one of the trials over which Nathaniel's grandfather had presided and had come to enquire about Mr Monkton's health. If so, then it was remarkable how quickly the news of the shooting had spread.

'I'm afraid my grandfather can't see anyone at present,' Nathaniel told him. 'He's not well.'

Simeon Makepeace shook his head. 'Begging your pardon, sir, but it's you I've come to see, not your grandfather.'

'Me?'

'Certainly. You see, I've read all about you in the newspapers. You're the fellow that can talk to ghosts, aren't you?'

Nathaniel shook his head. 'Not really. I've only seen one ghost and she didn't say a word.'

'All the same, you worked out what she wanted and carried out her wishes, didn't you?'

'You could say that.'

'Then you're the person I need to speak to. You see, I'm a haunted man, Master Wolfe.'

'I see. Well, perhaps you should start at the beginning.'

Simeon Makepeace nodded. 'I shall do my best, though it isn't always easy to know where a story starts exactly. But let's begin with my profession. I'm a solicitor's clerk.'

'And you work in London?'

'I do, sir. For the firm of Mordecai and Hemlock. Perhaps you've heard of them?'

Nathaniel shook his head.

'A well-respected firm, and I've been in their employ for nearly twenty-five years; firstly when old Mr Mordecai himself was in charge – splendid old gentleman he was – and then under Mr Hemlock, who is a very different sort of character altogether, but that's another story. My work consists mostly of copying up documents – letters, wills, statements, affidavits and so forth. The firm is not exactly over-staffed and there is a great deal for me to do. Often, I am required to stay at the office long into the night, copying the documents relating to a particular case.'

'That doesn't sound fair,' Nathaniel suggested.

Simeon Makepeace gave an apologetic smile. 'Dates of hearings are not easily changed, Master Wolfe. It is more economical to make the poor clerk work all through the night than to apply to the court for a new date. I understand that. After all, I am not a person of any great importance. No one bothers about me and I never bother about them. At least I never did before the old gentleman turned up.'

'What old gentleman?'

'I was coming to that. You see, there I was in my office one night. It must have been half past ten, but

I still had plenty of work to do. There wasn't a sound in the room except the scratching of my pen and the occasional rustle of paper. It was fairly chilly, for I had run out of coal an hour earlier, but I had my greatcoat and muffler on and I managed to continue. Then I noticed that it had suddenly got a great deal colder. Unnaturally cold, if you know what I mean?'

Simeon Makepeace looked eagerly at Nathaniel for some sign of recognition, and Nathaniel nodded. He was more than familiar with the chill that came from the other side of the grave and he knew how it turned your blood to ice. 'Go on,' he urged.

'Well, I looked up to see if the door had opened or something and there he was – an old, grey-haired man, standing there, staring right at me. Of course, I knew right away that he was a ghost. You can tell. I mean, it wasn't so much the way he looked, as how he made you feel. It was as if I was cast adrift on an ocean of loneliness, as though everything I'd ever known and loved was lost and gone and never going to return.'

'So what happened next?'

'Well, the old man held out his hand and I could see that on the palm of it was a ring, just a plain gold ring. He held it there like he wanted me to take it.'

'And did you?'

Simeon Makepeace shuddered and shook his head vigorously. 'Not me. No thank you! I wasn't having anything to do with it. I'm not a brave man, Master Wolfe, I don't mind admitting. I'm a solicitor's clerk, that's all. Dealing with ghosts is outside my line of experience.'

'So what *did* you do?'

'I picked up the bundle of documents that I was copying and flung them at him. Then I ran out of the room and didn't stop running until I got home again.'

'And was that the only time you saw this old man?'

'I wish it was. Since that night I've seen him on four further occasions, and each time it's been exactly the same. He stands there holding out the ring and looking expectant. It terrifies me.'

'Has anybody else seen him?'

Simeon Makepeace shook his head. 'Just me. At first my wife thought I was losing my mind and I was beginning to wonder myself if that wasn't true. Then, last week, she said she'd been talking about it with her mother, and her mother had said why not go and see that boy who was in the papers – Nathaniel Wolfe, that's his name. He talks to ghosts all the time, she said. It's nothing to him. He'll have the whole thing sorted out straightaway. And so here I am. You will help me out, won't you, Master Wolfe?'

Nathaniel sighed. 'I'd like to,' he said, 'but you've come at a very difficult time for me.'

'I'm not a rich man,' Simeon Makepeace continued,

'but if it's a question of money...' He put his hand inside his breast pocket.

Nathaniel shook his head. 'It's not the money,' he said. 'I have to look after my grandfather. He's very ill at the moment. In order to help you, I'd have to go to London, and I simply can't leave him right now. Besides, I think your mother-in-law may have an exaggerated idea of my powers. I can assure you, I do not talk to ghosts all the time.'

Simeon Makepeace looked wretched. 'You were my only hope, Master Wolfe,' he said. 'Don't say you're going to let me down.'

'I'm sorry,' Nathaniel replied. 'It just isn't possible.'

Simeon Makepeace gave a deep sigh and stood up. 'It was worth a try,' he said. Then he took out a dog-eared card which he handed to Nathaniel. 'This is my address, should you change your mind.'

Nathaniel took the card and thanked him. 'Perhaps you'd like to stay for breakfast?' he suggested.

But Simeon Makepeace shook his head. 'Thank you very much, but I have to get back. The work will be piling up. I'll show myself out. No need to make a fuss on my account. I'm a person of no importance, Master Wolfe. A person of no importance whatsoever.'

After Simeon Makepeace had left, Nathaniel stood in the parlour for a long time, wishing he could have answered differently. Finally, he sighed and put the matter out of his head. He would go and see how his grandfather was getting on, he decided.

He knocked lightly on the door of the drawing room then stepped inside. As he had expected, his grandfather was asleep, and Nathaniel was on the point of leaving once more when the old man's eyelids fluttered and he awoke. For a few moments he looked as if he had no idea where he was. Then, seeing Nathaniel, he smiled.

'Good morning, Grandad,' Nathaniel said. 'How are you today?'

'I'm all right as long as I stay perfectly still,' his grandfather said. 'When I move it feels as though someone has stuck a red hot poker into my shoulder. Still, I suppose I should consider myself lucky to be alive.'

'You certainly should,' Nathaniel agreed. 'If the bullet had gone just a couple of inches to the left, we might not be having this conversation.'

His grandfather nodded. 'You know, I had the strangest dream just now,' he said.

Nathaniel drew up a chair beside the couch and sat down. 'Tell me about it,' he said.

'I dreamt that I awoke in this room and felt very cold. There was a man standing next to the couch. I thought at first that he was the doctor, but then I saw he was a stranger. There was something very odd about him. I don't know how to explain it, exactly. It was as if he did not belong in this world. I know that sounds ridiculous, but I don't know how else to put it. I wondered, at first, if he were not Death himself, come to claim me. "What do you want?" I asked him. He said nothing, but he held out his hand and on the palm there was a ring. I think he wanted me to take it. Then all of a sudden he was gone and I was waking up again, properly this time, and you were standing there looking at me. I expect it was the drug that the doctor gave me.'

'I'm not so sure,' Nathaniel said. He told his grandfather about Simeon Makepeace's visit.

His grandfather listened carefully. 'It is quite clear what this means,' he said when Nathaniel had finished his tale. 'You must help this Simeon Makepeace.'

'But what about you, Grandad?' Nathaniel said. 'I need to stay here and look after you.'

Mr Monkton shook his head. 'James is perfectly capable of doing that, with a little help from Mrs McQuade. No, much as I hate to lose your company, Nathaniel, I believe you must go and resolve this matter. The spirit world is calling you back to itself and you must leave for London without delay.'

3. POPHAM'S PUPPET EMPORIUM

Lily Campion peered at the puppets in the window of the little toyshop on the corner of Wapping High Street. There were all kinds on display: soldiers, sailors, clowns, policemen, dogs, cats, bears and even elephants. Every inch of shelf-space was crammed with smiling or scowling faces made of wood or plaster or felt. Even though it was such a tiny store, Lily decided, it deserved its grand name, and it would certainly be the perfect place to buy a birthday present for the cook's niece. She opened the door and stepped inside.

Just twelve months ago, Lily had been working as a parlour maid in the household of Mr Chesterfield. It had not been a happy house and Lily was thoroughly miserable working there. Now, because of the part she had played in uncovering Mr Chesterfield's plot to poison his stepdaughter,

Sophie, she was no longer a maid but Sophie's companion. Her former master was dead. Miss Pemberton, an old friend of Sophie's mother, had been appointed Sophie's guardian and had moved into the house with them.

Now that she was a young lady instead of a parlour maid, Lily had more money at her disposal, and she had learned that one of the pleasures of having money was being able to spend it on other people.

When he heard the bell ring, the proprietor of Popham's Puppet Emporium emerged from a room behind the shop. He was an elderly man, slightly stooped, with an impressive white beard, like Father Christmas. 'How may I help you?' he asked.

'I was looking for a present for a little girl,' Lily told him.

The shopkeeper spread his arms wide to indicate his entire stock. 'Any of these puppets would be suitable for a little girl,' he replied. 'They are all hand-made from the finest materials.'

As Lily picked up a harlequin marionette and studied it, a girl of about six emerged from the room at the back of the shop.

'Hello,' she said.

'This is my granddaughter, Bella,' Mr Popham proudly announced.

'I'm very pleased to make your acquaintance,'

Lily told the little girl. 'My name is Lily.'

'Oh, I know that,' Bella replied, looking rather pleased with herself. 'Dimity told me you'd be coming.'

Lily was taken aback by this remark. 'Who is Dimity?' she asked.

Mr Popham smiled. 'Dimity is Bella's imaginary friend,' he explained.

Bella gave her grandfather a withering look. 'Dimity isn't imaginary,' she said. 'It's just that other people can't see him.'

'Oh, I understand,' Lily replied, with a wink at Mr Popham.

'If you think I can't see you winking, you must be very stupid,' Bella said scornfully.

'Bella! That was extremely rude,' Mr Popham declared. 'I want you to apologise immediately.'

'Sorry,' Bella said, reluctantly. Then she immediately disappeared back into the room behind the shop.

'I don't think she liked us making fun of her friend,' Lily said.

'She can be a bit difficult at times,' Mr Popham agreed. 'She misses her parents, I'm afraid.'

'Oh! Are they...?' Lily began.

Mr Popham shook his head. 'Only her father – my son, that is. He died of cholera.'

'I'm very sorry,' Lily said.

'It was five years ago now,' Mr Popham went on, 'and I have learned to live with it, though of course one never really gets over such a loss. Unfortunately, it has meant that Bella's mother has had to return to work. She went into service in a big house south of London. They wouldn't let her take Bella with her, so now she lives with me and only sees her mother at weekends.'

'I see. How sad for her!'

'Oh, Bella bears it well enough. She's a cheerful little thing and she enjoys helping me in the shop.'

Lily continued to examine the puppets for some time. At last she settled on the harlequin.

'Each puppet is made to order,' Mr Popham told her. 'The one on the shelf is for display purposes only. But I can have yours ready by the middle of next week.'

'That will be fine,' Lily said.

She left some money as a deposit. Then, just as she was about to leave, Bella suddenly reappeared. 'You need to tell your friend to hurry up about it,' she told Lily.

'What friend is that?' Lily asked.

'The one who can't do his buttons up,' Bella replied.

Lily laughed. Little children's heads are so full of

nonsense, she thought to herself. 'I'll do my best,' she told Bella. Then she set off for home.

When Lily opened the front door of Number 42 Chudleigh Street, the first thing she heard was a peal of laughter. Oh, good! We have a visitor! she said to herself, for she was a sociable individual. As a parlour maid, she had enjoyed the camaraderie of the servants' quarters, even if she had often complained about the workload. In her new position as a young lady, she sometimes found that she missed the free and easy chat of the world below stairs.

She opened the door to the front parlour and found, to her delight, that their visitor was none other than her old friend, Nathaniel. He stood up, smiling broadly, when he saw her.

'What are you doing back in London?' she asked, when they had exchanged greetings.

'He's ghost-hunting again,' Sophie said.

Lily raised one eyebrow. 'I would have thought you'd have had enough of that,' she observed.

'I *have* had enough of it,' Nathaniel replied, 'but it hasn't had enough of me.' He described Simeon Makepeace's visit and his grandfather's dream.

'So what are you going to do about it?' Lily asked when he had reached the end of his tale.

'I've written to Mr Makepeace to say that I shall be

visiting him in his office tonight,' Nathaniel replied.

'Well, in that case, I'll come with you,' Lily announced.

Nathaniel grinned delightedly. 'I was hoping you'd say that,' he told her.

'I'll come too, if you like,' Sophie said, but she spoke without much enthusiasm.

Miss Pemberton frowned anxiously. 'I'm not sure…' she began.

Nathaniel laughed. 'That's all right,' he said. 'Sophie doesn't have to come. Lily and I are used to seeing ghosts, but it's not everyone's cup of tea.'

Sophie looked relieved. She wanted very much to be brave, but growing up as a young lady meant she had led a sheltered life, and she found it hard to break free of the restrictions this imposed on her.

'Where are you staying in London?' Miss Pemberton asked.

Nathaniel gave the name of the inn where he had lodged that morning.

Miss Pemberton shook her head. 'You must stay here with us,' she said.

'Yes, please do!' the others urged him.

Nathaniel did not need much persuading.

'We'll arrange for your bags to be sent over in a cab,' Miss Pemberton declared. 'Then, over dinner, you can tell us all about your new life in the country.'

*

Sharing a meal with Lily, Sophie and Miss Pemberton was an altogether more pleasant affair than dining with Lord and Lady Huntercombe. There were not so many courses to eat, but a great deal more laughter, as Nathaniel proceeded to imitate some of the grand people he had encountered in the last twelve months. But the mood soon changed when he described the bodysnatchers he and his grandfather had surprised in the cemetery.

'It's happening everywhere,' Miss Pemberton told him. 'If the papers are to be believed, there is not a graveyard in London that is safe.'

'But what can be done about it?' Sophie asked.

'That's obvious,' Lily said. 'They have to find the people responsible and lock them up.'

'Easier said than done,' Nathaniel pointed out. 'They are the sort who are prepared to stop at nothing. But for a stroke of luck, I would have been dead now, instead of sitting here, talking to you.'

When the meal was finally over it was time for Nathaniel and Lily to set out for Simeon Makepeace's office.

'You will take care, won't you?' Miss Pemberton asked.

'Of course we will,' Nathaniel told her. He put on his coat and turned to Lily. 'Are you ready?' he asked.

'Nathaniel!' Sophie said, giggling. 'You've buttoned up your coat all wrong.'

Lily gasped, for she immediately recalled the words of Bella Popham. *Tell your friend to hurry up about it...the one who can't do his buttons up.*

No one else noticed her reaction. Nathaniel simply looked down at his coat and smiled. 'So I have,' he said. 'I'm afraid I'll never make a proper gentleman.'

Perhaps it was just a coincidence, Lily told herself, as she followed Nathaniel out of the front door. Even so, it was very strange. She made up her mind that she would have another chat with Bella Popham before too long.

4. THE DOOR IN THE ROCK

It was eight o'clock when they stepped out of the front door. Already the sky was growing dark, and for the last hour fog had been creeping steadily up from the river, casting its ghostly shroud over the city. Against this murky conspiracy, the feeble glow of the gas lights was all but powerless.

Lily shivered and clutched at the collars of her coat. 'Not a night to linger on street corners,' she observed.

Nathaniel nodded and looked up and down the street for a hansom cab. He had seen the underside of the city at close quarters and knew that on a night such as this an unseen army of pickpockets, street-robbers, mug-hunters, cut-throats and common vagabonds waited in the shadows, ready to pounce on their unsuspecting victims. Fortunately, at that moment a cab came clattering over the cobbles, and pulled up beside them.

They gave the driver the address and climbed into the carriage. As it jerked into motion, Nathaniel felt a thrill of pleasure. They were heading for an appointment with a haunted man. It was not something that many people would look forward to. But this was the life that had beckoned to him from the security of his grandfather's cottage in the countryside. And he had answered the call, because the city was in his blood, and because, whether he liked it or not, London had chosen him as its ghost-hunter.

After some time the driver stopped and they clambered out to find themselves in a narrow passage where the buildings seemed to lean together, as if to whisper to one another. A brass plate advertising the offices of Messrs Mordecai and Hemlock was just visible in the gloom. Nathaniel knocked on the door and after some delay it was opened by Simeon Makepeace, clutching a candlestick in one hand. He led them up a narrow staircase to the room in which he worked.

It was unfurnished except for a rickety wooden chair and a desk piled high with bundles of manuscripts tied up with string. Ranged around the floor were other, similar stacks of documents, giving the room the appearance of a left-luggage office where no one had arrived to claim their abandoned belongings for years. It was not possible to see much of the decoration, because the light was limited to the single candle that Simeon Makepeace clutched in his hand and the glow cast by a feeble-looking fire. Nevertheless, it was clear that the room was festooned with cobwebs, that plaster was coming away from the walls, and that a smell of damp hung so thickly in the air that it caught at the back of your throat.

Makepeace saw them glancing around the room and looked embarrassed. 'Not much to boast about, I'm afraid,' he said apologetically. 'Mr Hemlock doesn't believe in wasting money. I would say, make yourselves comfortable, but...'

'It's all right,' Nathaniel told him. 'I've put up with worse.' He sat down in a corner of the room and Lily sat beside him. 'You just carry on with your work, Mr Makepeace. We'll wait and see whether the old gentleman with the ring will grace us with his presence tonight.'

Time passed very slowly in Simeon Makepeace's office, and after a while Nathaniel must have dropped off to sleep. He awoke to a dig in the ribs from Lily and immediately noticed two things: the scratching of Simeon Makepeace's pen had stopped and the room had become very much colder.

It was not just the ordinary coldness of a room at midnight in late March. It was the cold of death itself, and along with it came a terrible feeling of loneliness. Although there were two other people in the room with him, Nathaniel felt as if he were standing alone on a cliff top, looking down upon an everlasting sea of cold grey water. As he was thinking this, a figure began to take shape in the corner of the room.

At first it was no more than a column of mist, but gradually it assumed the form of an elderly man whose eyes were fixed on Nathaniel's. Slowly, the old man held out his hand, and Nathaniel saw that, just as Simeon Makepeace had described, there was a ring resting on his palm. He wants me to take it, Nathaniel thought to himself. Very well then, that's what I'll do.

But it was easier said than done. His body did not want to co-operate. It was as if, at some deep instinctive level, it knew this danger should not be approached. Nathaniel had to use all his willpower to force himself to walk the short distance across the room. At last he stood directly in front of the old man and reached out to take the ring.

Immediately, he felt the old man's hand close around his in a grip like iron. Instantly, Simeon Makepeace's office vanished and Nathaniel found himself standing in a narrow passage, the floor, walls and ceiling of which were all made of rock. Slime dripped down the sides and rats scurried away into the echoing darkness.

'Where am I?' Nathaniel cried out.

But the old man made no answer. Still clutching Nathaniel's hand, he led the way along the corridor, and Nathaniel found that he was compelled to follow.

It was a passage that seemed to have no end – the sort of place in which one finds oneself lost in the worst kind of nightmare. But this was no nightmare. It was as real and as terrible as anything Nathaniel had ever endured.

On and on the old man went. From time to time Nathaniel glimpsed wooden doors set into the rock, studded with nails and reinforced with great iron bands. From behind these doors came the unmistakable sound of moaning and sobbing, as if someone were being tortured within, but the old man took no notice, merely pulling Nathaniel along at an even greater pace.

It was bitterly cold in that dreadful place, but that was nothing to the stench. As a boy, trying to earn money for food, Nathaniel had cleared up the filth left behind in the markets and eating-houses of London. He had seen more than enough rotting meat and fish guts to last a lifetime, carried buckets of the stuff back and forth all day long. He had been down in the sewers below the city where the waste of thousands of bodies was deposited daily, until it became an underground river so foul and so contaminated that it ate through the very bricks from which the waterways were constructed. Yet he had never smelled anything like this. It was an odour of decay and corruption as strong as if he had come to the very heart of death itself.

This must be hell, he thought to himself. From what he had heard from the preachers who sometimes stood on street corners in London, shouting about the world to come, he had expected hell to be a place of fire and brimstone. But this narrow passage was cold, not hot. Cold enough to stop the blood from flowing in your veins. Nevertheless, Nathaniel was certain that he was right. This was the place where everything bad had its origin, where the mistakes and wrong turnings that people made in their lives reached their ultimate conclusion.

At last the old man came to a halt in front of one of the thick wooden doors set in the rock. Still without relaxing his grip on Nathaniel for one second, he put his other hand in his pocket and drew out a bunch of keys. He fitted one of these into the lock and the door opened with a hideous groan. Inside, Nathaniel glimpsed a space no larger than a small cupboard, which had been hollowed out of the bare rock.

He turned to the old man. 'Why are you showing me this?' he demanded. 'I don't understand what I'm here for.'

Instead of replying, the old man seized Nathaniel's throat, and for a moment Nathaniel thought he was going to be killed. Then, abruptly, he found himself propelled into the niche in the rock, and the door was shut behind him with a resounding clang. A moment later he heard the key turn in the lock. Now, at last, he understood the old man's purpose in bringing him here. He was to be held prisoner.

In that narrow space, there was only just room to stand upright and no room at all to turn or stretch out his arms. Nathaniel had always had a horror of confined spaces, and now that he was trapped like an animal in a snare, he felt that horror rise within him to an almost unbearable pitch. He began to shiver uncontrollably as panic gripped his body. I will be imprisoned here for the rest of eternity, he told himself. I will never again breathe fresh air, never feel the sun on my face, never see my friends.

Yet even that was not the hardest thing to bear. Much worse was the sense that something important had been left undone. He did not know what it was. Indeed, he suspected that it was nothing whatsoever to do with him. It was some task which the old man had failed to complete in his lifetime. But the awareness of that unfulfilled commitment was the real torment. It ate into Nathaniel's soul, more savagely than the cold or the dark, the stench or the cramp. It was like a pain that begins as a slight ache behind one eye but gradually becomes stronger and stronger until it feels as if someone is pushing a needle through the side of your head. It consumed Nathaniel, a cold fire that would burn down the centuries, a pain so great he longed to die so that it would stop. It was too much for him. He opened his mouth and screamed.

'Nathaniel, stop it!'

He felt a stinging pain across his face, opened his eyes and found himself back in the solicitor's office. Simeon Makepeace and Lily were staring at him and he realised that Lily had just slapped him. He wanted to sob with relief.

'What happened?' Lily demanded.

Nathaniel thought about it. How could he describe the misery that he had just witnessed? 'I saw the hell which that old man inhabits,' he said at last. 'I believe I shared it for a moment. I don't know what he has done to deserve this punishment but I do know this much. Whatever it takes, no matter what the risk, I must do my best to release him from that unspeakable torment.'

5. THE DELVER

The next morning, when Nathaniel awoke and found himself lying in a strange bed, he was at first bewildered. Then he recalled that he was staying with Sophie, Lily and Miss Pemberton. With that recollection came the memory of the events at the solicitor's office. He shuddered at the thought of the brief but terrible moments he had spent imprisoned in the cubby-hole in the rock, and the burning awareness the experience had given him of some appalling wrong he was powerless to put right. No wonder the old man had taken to haunting people.

The previous night, though he had finally understood that he was not condemned to spend the rest of his life locked away in a cell underground, he had still been in no fit state to discuss what he had seen. So Simeon Makepeace had agreed to call on them the next morning after breakfast. Nathaniel looked at the bedside clock. It was already nine o'clock. He had better hurry, he realised, or he would have had nothing to eat before the clerk arrived.

He got out of bed and drew back the curtains. The sun came streaming into the room, defying him to feel gloomy. He opened the window and put his head outside. At the corner of the street an organ-grinder was cranking out a tune. Nearer at hand a paper-boy was yelling the news. Carriage wheels clattered across the cobblestones, costermongers called out their wares, church bells rang, dogs barked, horses neighed, gangs of ragged street children chased each other back and forth between the alleyways. Nathaniel found himself smiling. Despite what had happened the previous night, it still felt good to be back in London.

After he had washed, he got dressed and went downstairs to find Lily, Sophie and Miss Pemberton already seated at the breakfast table.

'About time you got up,' Lily said, as Nathaniel sat down and poured himself a cup of tea.

'I was tired,' Nathaniel told her. 'You've no idea how exhausting it is to change places with a ghost.'

'Is that what really happened?' Sophie asked, her eyes wide with astonishment. 'You actually experienced what it feels like to be that poor old man?'

'Yes, I believe I did.'

'Then what are you going to do next?'

'Well, first of all we have to find out who the old

man is,' Nathaniel replied, 'or perhaps, I should say, who he was. And I'm hoping that Simeon Makepeace will be able to shed some light on that this morning.'

'Then you had better stop talking and start eating,' Miss Pemberton said, 'for I suspect he will be with us very shortly.'

Miss Pemberton's prediction proved true, and Nathaniel was only halfway through a plate of bacon and eggs when George, the footman, announced that Simeon Makepeace had arrived. With reluctance, Nathaniel abandoned his breakfast and followed the others into the parlour.

Simeon Makepeace bowed several times to each of the ladies and shook Nathaniel by the hand. 'I do hope you have recovered from your ordeal of last night,' he said when they were all sitting down at last.

'Quite recovered, thank you,' Nathaniel told him. 'But I know enough about these things to realise that the old man will be back unless we can discover what's troubling him and do something about it. He won't rest, and he won't let us rest, either. So we need to begin by finding out who he is. There must be something more that you can tell us.'

Simeon Makepeace sighed. 'I wish I could,' he said, 'but I'd never set eyes on him until he turned up in my office, holding out his ring like that, and I haven't the slightest idea why he should choose to appear to someone so insignificant as me.'

'Perhaps it has something to do with your work,' Lily suggested. 'Do you remember exactly what you were doing the very first time he appeared?'

'Well, I was copying up a document, obviously,' Simeon Makepeace replied, 'since that's all I ever do.'

'Can you remember which document?'

Simeon Makepeace shook his head. 'The thing is, Miss, you saw the effect the old man had on Master Nathaniel. Well, I was no better. I just picked up the pile of manuscripts from my desk, threw them in his direction, then ran off home. It was Mr Hemlock who found them the next day. He wasn't very pleased that the documents were all over the floor, I can tell you. I said I'd finish the job that morning if he gave me back the documents, but he insisted they were all complete, though I could have sworn I was halfway through copying up a letter.'

'Did you explain what had happened?' Nathaniel asked.

'I tried to, of course, but he said I must have been dreaming, and warned me that if he found any more manuscripts tossed around the room, I'd be out on my ear.'

'And you're certain you can't remember anything about the document you were working on when the ghost appeared?'

'Well, afterwards, when I thought it over, the name Cedric Melville seemed to ring a bell. So I mentioned it to Mr Hemlock later that morning. I said, "Begging your pardon, sir, but wasn't there a letter to a Sir Cedric Melville that needed finishing off?" But he said he didn't know what I was talking about.'

'Perhaps you got it wrong?' Lily suggested.

Simeon Makepeace shrugged. 'Perhaps I did. But the funny thing is, when I went into his office that afternoon to hand him some correspondence, there was a file on the desk in front of him. There was just a moment before he put another file down on top of it so I only caught the briefest glimpse, but I could have sworn the name on the front was Cedric Melville. Then Mr Hemlock picked the two of them up together and put them in the locked cabinet behind his desk.'

'Couldn't you try to sneak a look in the cabinet when Mr Hemlock isn't there?' Nathaniel asked.

Simeon Makepeace shook his head. 'He keeps his keys in the drawer in his desk,' he said. 'Takes them with him whenever he leaves the building. Besides, I'd lose my job if he caught me.'

'What about the other partner – Mr Mordecai?' Miss Pemberton asked.

'Mr Mordecai doesn't come into the office much these days,' Makepeace replied. 'Ever since his wife died he's lost interest in his work. They were a very devoted couple, I believe. He does a bit of work from his home in Greenwich, but that's all, more's the pity. Things were different when he was in charge. A very decent man, he was, and that's something you can't say about Mr Hemlock, the old skinflint.'

Simeon Makepeace took an envelope out of his pocket. 'This is all the money I can spare,' he said. He held it out to Nathaniel. 'I'm trusting you to use it if you need to. Just give me back my peace of mind. That's all I ask.'

'Well, that wasn't very enlightening,' Lily said, after Simeon Makepeace had gone. 'Where do we go from here?'

Nathaniel thought about it for a while. Then he grinned and said, 'I think I'll go and have a chat with my old pal, Jeremiah. He's always helped me in the past when I haven't known which way to turn.'

Jeremiah was a tosher, one of those who worked beneath the streets of London in the everlasting struggle to keep the sewers from getting blocked up. When Nathaniel had lived with his father in Mrs Bizzantine's East End lodging house, Jeremiah had occupied a room on the ground floor. There were those, like Nathaniel's father, who refused to have anything to do with Jeremiah, because the smell of the sewers never left him. But Nathaniel had always found him to be a trusty friend.

When Nathaniel turned up at Mrs Bizzantine's house an hour later, his old landlady seemed delighted to see him.

'My word, Master Wolfe, I didn't expect to see you again,' she told him, curtseying and bowing as if he were the Lord Mayor of London, 'what with you being so famous now and a proper gentleman as well. I must say it's a great honour to have you paying us a visit, a very great honour indeed.'

Nathaniel took all this with a pinch of salt. He knew that the only thing Mrs Bizzantine really respected was money. When he had been poor, she had regularly threatened to throw him and his father out onto the street whenever the rent was late. All this new-found delight was just in case he might be able to put some extra pennies her way.

'It's Jeremiah I've come to see,' he told her.

'Of course, Master Wolfe. That's the right attitude. Don't forget your old friends, those what stood by you when times were hard. You go ahead and knock on his door. I'm sure he'll be as pleased as Punch to see you.'

That much was true, at least. It was all the same to Jeremiah whether Nathaniel was a gentleman or a pauper. He grinned from ear to ear when he saw his old friend and shook him so vigorously by the hand that Nathaniel thought there was a real danger his arm might come loose if the shaking carried on much longer.

'Come on in and make yourself at home,' Jeremiah said.

The tosher's room was no bigger than the pantry in Mr Monkton's house, but it suited Jeremiah well enough, for he had very few possessions to clutter it up: a couple of chairs, a table and a mattress, a plain wooden box, and in a corner of the room, a cage filled with rats.

Catching rats was a sideline of Jeremiah's. The sewers were full of them, of course, and Jeremiah sold those he caught to the owner of the George and Dragon in Shadwell, who staged ratting competitions. Those who were fond of a wager brought their dogs along to see whose animal could catch the most rats. It was a savage sport, but London was a savage place if you looked beneath the surface. Nathaniel took no notice of the rats, though their eyes gleamed and they squealed excitedly when he came too close to their cage.

'I'm here to ask your advice, Jeremiah,' Nathaniel said, when they had shut the door and were safe from the eager ears of Mrs Bizzantine.

'In that case, I shall have to light my pipe,' Jeremiah said. 'Once I've got a bit of a smoke on the go, I find my brain works a whole lot better.' He took out his pipe and tobacco pouch, and while Nathaniel described the visit of Simeon Makepeace, Jeremiah blew a succession of smoke rings, each one bigger and grander than the last. He listened attentively to Nathaniel's story, asking only the occasional question when he wanted to be sure of a detail. At the end he shook his head.

'Its a difficult matter, Nat, and no mistake. Ghosts and whatnot. To tell you the truth, it's beyond my reckoning altogether. But I'll tell you what we'll do. We'll ask the rats.'

Nathaniel nodded. It was exactly what he had expected, for he had seen Jeremiah's method of decision-making in action before. The tosher was a great believer in the wisdom of rats. 'They don't work for a living, do they?' he had once asked Nathaniel. 'They let us do the work and then, when we're not looking, they comes along and takes whatever they fancies. You have to be smart to get away with that.'

On the previous occasion he had placed one of the animals in a wooden box from which there were two possible exits. If the rat chose to exit from the first entrance, Jeremiah took it to mean 'yes'; if it chose the second exit, Jeremiah took it to mean 'no'.

'But what question shall we ask them that can only

be answered with a simple yes or no?' Nathaniel asked.

Jeremiah tapped the side of his nose with his finger. 'I see you're thinking of my old method, Nat. But I've improved greatly upon that. Take a look at my latest decision-maker.'

He picked up the wooden box that had been standing against the wall and held it up proudly. 'See. There's four exits now. All equally difficult to find. Which means that we can ask Mr Rat anything we like. Come on, let's go outside and I'll show you how it works. You'd better carry this. I'll take the cage.'

They went outside and Nathaniel set the wooden box down in the middle of the cobbled yard, as Jeremiah directed him.

'As I've already said,' Jeremiah went on, 'there are now four holes in the box. Out of one of these Mr Rat will exit. But what will that tell us, eh?'

He looked at Nathaniel, who only shrugged.

'Here comes the stroke of genius,' Jeremiah continued, 'even if I do say so myself.' He put his hand in his pocket and drew out four playing cards, which he held up for Nathaniel's inspection. 'The ace of hearts,' Jeremiah announced, 'standing, as you might imagine, for matters of love. The ace of diamonds, meaning money, wealth and property.

The ace of spades, signifying work of all kinds. And the ace of clubs, which is a token for violence. Now then, we lays one of these cards on the ground next to each of the four holes. Next, we introduces our whiskery friend into the maze. If you would be so kind as to lift the flap on the other side of the box and tilt it upwards, Nat. Then you can slide it down again smartly once I've popped our friend inside.'

Putting on thick leather gauntlets, Jeremiah carefully opened the wire cage. Sensing that freedom was close at hand, the rats began squeaking excitedly and trying their best to escape. But Jeremiah was too quick for them. He picked up a solitary rat with one hand and swiftly brought the lid down again with the other.

'Now then, my beauty,' Jeremiah said, gripping the rat firmly by the scruff of its neck, so that no matter how it struggled it could not turn and bite him, 'young Nathaniel here's got a question he wants you to answer. So listen carefully. He's being haunted, see, by the ghost of an old man what holds out a ring on the palm of his hand, and he wants you to tell him what lies at the heart of the mystery.'

He turned to Nathaniel. 'Are you ready?'

'Yes.'

'Then in he goes,' Jeremiah said, deftly slipping the struggling rat through the entrance hole.

Nathaniel slid the wooden panel back into place and settled the box upon the ground.

'Do you really think this will work?' he asked, as they listened to the rat scrabbling about in the interior of the box.

'Never been more certain of anything in me life,' Jeremiah assured him. 'Rats know everything that's going on, you see. Stands to reason. They're everywhere, even if you can't see them, and they all talks to one another. If you was to stand silently down in the sewers, as I do, you would hear them, passing the news from one to another like thousands of gossiping fishwives. They're...'

But he did not finish his sentence, for just at that moment the rat's snout poked nervously from one of the exit holes. For a moment it hesitated, whiskers twitching. Then it shot out of the box, ran across the yard and disappeared.

Jeremiah bent down and picked up the ace of hearts. He nodded. 'So it's a matter of love. Well, I suppose that was only to be expected, what with the ghost holding out a ring and all. Someone's been jilted, that's clear enough, though whether your ghost was the one what got jilted or the one what did the jilting, that's another question.'

'What do you suggest I do now?' Nathaniel asked.

Jeremiah thought about this for a moment. Then

he nodded. 'I think we need to go and have a word with Milky Melchy,' he said.

'Milky Melchy?' Nathaniel repeated. 'Who's he?'

'Milky Melchy is what they call a delver,' Jeremiah replied. 'He finds things for people.'

'What sort of things?'

'All sorts. Stolen goods, missing documents, urgent information. But most of all he specialises in tracking down people – those what have been kidnapped and those what have disappeared of their own free will. Decent folks, petty crooks or out-and-out villains. He sniffs them all out. They do say that some very well-known people have consulted him. It's rumoured he discovered where the wife of a Member of Parliament was hiding. And I wouldn't be surprised, neither, for some of them high and mighty folks gets up to worse villainy than your ordinary, everyday criminal. But true or not, Melchy wouldn't breathe a word about it. He keeps his secrets and that's why people trust him.'

Where can I find him?' Nathaniel asked.

'In his office above a tailor's shop in the Whitechapel Road,' Jeremiah replied. 'We can go there now, if you like.'

'Thanks, Jeremiah,' Nathaniel said. 'I knew I could rely on you.'

They put the cage of rats and the wooden box back

in Jeremiah's room, then set off together to find the delver.

'So why is he called Milky Melchy?' Nathaniel asked, as they made their way through the narrow streets towards Whitechapel.

'Well, his full name is Melchisedec, which is a bit of a mouthful,' Jeremiah said, 'and they call him Milky on account of his pale complexion. They do say that he never leaves his office except at night.'

'But if that's true, then how does he find things out?' Nathaniel replied.

'Ah, that's the beauty of Melchy's method,' Jeremiah replied. 'He's got an army of fishers working for him.'

'Fishers?'

'Earwiggers, tattlers, whisperers, informers – call them what you like. There's nearly as many people passing on scraps of news to Milky Melchy as there are rats down the sewers.'

'I see.'

'There are those as lives on nothing else but what Melchy pays them for fishing. Anyhow, you'll see for yourself in a minute, 'cos we're here now.'

They had stopped outside a tailor's shop. Beside the store was a door leading to the upper storey and a notice above the knocker read, *Melchisedec Rosenberg, Enquiries Conducted.* Jeremiah knocked twice and the door was opened by a short man with a patch over one eye, a shaven head and a little pointed beard that gave him a slightly devilish appearance. 'We've come to see Mr Rosenberg,' Jeremiah told him.

'Selling information or looking for it?' the man asked.

'Looking for it.'

'Then you'd best follow me.'

As he led the way up a flight of stairs, Nathaniel noticed that one of the man's legs was significantly shorter than the other. To compensate for this, the shoe of that foot was heavily built up, but he moved rapidly, despite his disability. An assortment of street-urchins, beggars, and down and outs of every variety sat on the stairs, waiting for their chance to try to sell some scrap of gossip. They regarded the newcomers curiously but made no comment. Hours of hanging around the delver's office had clearly taught them patience.

At the top of the stairs, Nathaniel and Jeremiah were shown into Milky Melchy's office. In contrast to Simeon Makepeace's place of work, this was a very tidy room. Against one wall was a wooden cabinet containing a large number of drawers, each one labelled with a letter of the alphabet. In front of the cabinet was Milky Melchy's desk, on which there were several leather-bound memorandum books.

He was writing in one of these as they entered.

Milky Melchy himself was tall, thin and, as expected, remarkably pale, with long black hair which hung in ringlets about his shoulders. Despite the fire burning brightly in the grate, he wore a fur overcoat and a cravat.

He put down his pen and regarded them out of liquid dark eyes that reminded Nathaniel of a spaniel Mrs Bizzantine had once possessed. 'Well Jeremiah,' he said, 'it's a pleasure to see you again. And this is...?'

'Nathaniel Wolfe,' Jeremiah replied.

'Pleased to make your acquaintance, Master Wolfe. How can I help you two gentlemen?'

'I'm looking for information about someone called Cedric Melville,' Nathaniel explained.

Milky Melchy got up and went over to his cabinet. He pulled out the drawer labelled M and searched through a great wad of small cards. Finally, he turned back to face them and shook his head. 'He's not in my records,' he said. 'But I could make some enquiries.'

'How much would it cost?' Nathaniel asked.

Milky Melchy named a fairly modest sum.

Nathaniel nodded. 'Will it take long?'

'That depends. It might take no time at all. It might take weeks. But if he exists, or existed once, then I'll find him.'

'How can you be so sure?'

The ghost of a smile flickered across Milky Melchy's face. 'Every individual who walks across the face of this earth leaves footprints, Master Wolfe,' he replied. 'He may not realise it; or he may take great care to erase those footprints as he goes. Either way, it makes no difference, for he can never remove every trace. If you know where to look and you look hard enough, you'll see the record of his passing. And that's my job. I look, I listen and I ask questions. I lift up stones and I delve into places other people will not go. Sooner or later I always find the answers. So don't you fret. I'll dig him out for and you'll hear from my assistant, Mr Tibbs, just as soon as I've got some news. In the meantime, I'll bid you good day.'

They left the office and made their way downstairs, walking past the queue of Milky Melchy's informants once more.

'What would you say to a spot of refreshment?' Jeremiah asked when they were back on the street.

'I'd say it was a good idea,' Nathaniel replied.

'Then I suggest we repair to the Nag's Head on the corner of Whitechapel Road, and have ourselves something to drink and a couple of meat pies.'

The Nag's Head was a great heaving gin palace, and it was packed to the rafters with customers. Blacksmiths and bootmakers, sailors and shopkeepers, roadsweepers, railwaymen and rent collectors all slaked their thirsts side-by-side. Jeremiah spied an empty table in the corner and they edged their way through the crowd towards it. Halfway there, Nathaniel was elbowed aside by a cabbie staggering drunkenly towards the exit. As a result, Nathaniel bumped into the man standing beside him, causing him to spill his drink. The man turned on him furiously.

'What the hell do you think you're playing at?' he demanded.

Jeremiah immediately stepped between them. 'Just an accident, my friend,' he said gently. 'No cause to go losing our tempers.' He put out his hand and stopped a barman who was passing with a tray of drinks. 'A pint of ale for this gentleman,' he said, 'and two meat pies for myself and my friend here. We'll be over in the corner.'

The man who had spilt his drink merely grunted and returned to his conversation. Jeremiah and Nathaniel continued on their way towards the empty table. But Nathaniel couldn't help feeling that there was something familiar about the man. Where had he seen him before?

'Thanks very much for intervening just now,' Nathaniel said, when they were finally sitting down.

'He was an ugly-looking customer,' Jeremiah replied. 'So I thought it best to keep him sweet – if the likes of him can ever truly be called sweet. Anyhow, tell us what you thought of Milky Melchy.'

'I liked him,' Nathaniel said.

'There are those who won't have anything to do with him, on account of him being Jewish,' Jeremiah said, 'but I didn't think you'd be of that opinion.'

'Of course not,' Nathaniel replied. If there was one thing that growing up in the East End of London had taught him, it was that you got good and bad people of all kinds, colours and creeds.

'Good,' Jeremiah said, 'because I've a very high opinion of him myself. He helped me find my old dad what I hadn't seen for nearly thirty years and what was at death's door. Didn't charge me a packet, neither.'

The barman came over with their pies just then, and for a moment they were too busy eating to talk any further. It was a long time since Nathaniel had tasted a proper London meat pie and he realised that, for all the fine food in his grandfather's house, it was something he had really missed.

'What I want to know,' Jeremiah continued when they had both eaten up every last crumb, 'is why you can't simply ask the old man with the ring who he is and what he wants?'

'He doesn't speak,' Nathaniel explained. 'Neither did the ghost of Mrs Chesterfield, come to that.

Perhaps ghosts can't speak to the living. Maybe they aren't allowed. Or maybe a person is like a book with only so many words in them, and once all those words are used up...'

He stopped suddenly. On the other side of the room the man who had spilt his drink had turned his head to speak to an acquaintance, and Nathaniel could plainly see that his right ear was dreadfully mutilated.

'It's the graverobber!' he cried. He sprang to his feet and tried to force his way through the crowd. But even while they had been sitting at the table eating their meat pies, the place had filled up still further. It was a real struggle to make headway. As he pushed forwards, the bodysnatcher finished his drink, and headed for the exit. Desperately, Nathaniel fought to catch up with him. But it was no good. By the time Nathaniel had followed him out onto the street, the bodysnatcher had vanished.

6. THE BLACK DROP

The next morning Nathaniel came down to breakfast to find a letter from his grandfather waiting for him. He wasted no time in opening it.

Dear Nathaniel,

I am writing to let you know that I am greatly improved. You need have no further worries about me. James has been looking after me extremely capably. Indeed, I am very much hoping I will be allowed out of bed for an hour or two tomorrow morning. I cannot tell you how dull I find the life of an invalid.

Nathaniel smiled to himself. His grandfather was used to leading an active life with plenty of physical exercise. No doubt he found it very hard to adjust to being a bed-bound patient.

I am happy to inform you that there have been no more outbreaks of bodysnatching in the county. Lord Huntercombe came to see me yesterday and he is of the opinion that the villains may have removed themselves to London.

Perhaps his lordship was not quite the blockhead that Nathaniel had imagined him to be.

Lady Huntercombe is not so sure. She suspects they may be still in the neighbourhood. I believe she feels I should have done more to apprehend them in the churchyard, though of course she does not say as much.

Nathaniel made a face. He would have liked to see Lady Huntercombe facing a loaded pistol. He looked up from his letter to see the others watching him anxiously.

'I hope it is not bad news?' Miss Pemberton enquired.

Nathaniel shook his head. 'My grandfather writes to say that he is getting better,' he informed her.

'I am glad to hear it,' Miss Pemberton declared.

Nathaniel returned to his letter.

I have dreamt about that strange old man again, only this time he was not holding a ring but an hourglass. He held it aloft to show me how quickly the sands were running out and I was left in no doubt about his meaning. Whatever he wishes you to do, there is not much time to achieve it. He looked at me with eyes that were so full of sadness and urgency that my heart bled for him. I hope and trust that you will be the means of relieving that poor soul of whatever terrible burden afflicts him and I look forward to seeing you back here safe and sound.

With fondest wishes,
Your loving grandfather

Nathaniel put the letter in his pocket and helped himself to some toast. It was all very well to talk about time running out, but before he could help the old man he had to solve the mystery of who he was and what he meant by holding out that ring.

After breakfast Miss Pemberton announced that she had to attend the funeral of an old friend. Sophie offered to go with her to the railway station to see her off, leaving Lily and Nathaniel by themselves.

'I have to visit a toy shop to collect a present for the cook's niece,' Lily told Nathaniel. 'I'd like you to come with me.'

Nathaniel looked sceptical. 'I don't know much about buying presents for little children,' he said.

'You needn't worry about that. The present has already been chosen,' Lily told him. 'I just want you to meet the granddaughter of the man who owns the shop.' She described her previous visit to Popham's Puppet Emporium and Bella's parting comment that she should tell her friend who couldn't do up his buttons to hurry up. 'And then, that night, when we set off for Simeon Makepeace's office, you buttoned up your coat wrongly. Remember?'

'So what does that prove?' Nathaniel asked.

'I've absolutely no idea,' Lily said. 'I just thought it might be worth you meeting her yourself.'

Nathaniel shrugged. 'Well, I've got nothing better to do,' he admitted.

So they set out together for Popham's Puppet Emporium, but when they reached the shop, they found a sign in the window advertising a closing-down sale. 'Oh, what a pity!' Lily exclaimed. 'It's such a nice shop.' She pushed the door open and stepped inside.

Mr Popham appeared from the room behind the shop and smiled when he saw his customers. 'Miss Lily, isn't it?' he said.

Lily nodded and introduced Nathaniel.

'Your harlequin is ready,' Mr Popham said, taking it out from a drawer to show her.

'It's lovely!' Lily said.

'Then I'll put it in a box for you.'

'Thank you.'

Mr Popham wrapped the puppet in several layers of tissue paper and placed it carefully in a cardboard box.

I'm sorry to see that you're closing down,' Lily told him, as she handed over the rest of the money.

'Well, it's not as if I want to,' Mr Popham replied, wistfully. 'But the landlord has doubled the rent overnight. So there's nothing I can do.'

'What will happen to you?'

Mr Popham shrugged and handed over the box. 'Who knows, my dear? No doubt I'll survive, somehow or other.' Then he dropped his voice to a whisper. 'It's little Bella I'm worried about. She can't go to her mother because they won't have children in the house where she works, and when I'm turned out of the shop I don't know what will become of her.'

'That's terrible!' Lily said.

'Well, we needn't despair just yet,' Mr Popham continued. 'Something may turn up.'

Just then the little girl herself appeared.

'Do you remember Miss Lily, Bella?' her grandfather asked.

Bella nodded. 'Yes, of course I do.'

'And this is her friend, Nathaniel.'

'Pleased to make your acquaintance,' Nathaniel said.

Bella frowned at him. 'Have you found Albert yet?' she demanded.

'Who is Albert?' Nathaniel asked, rather taken aback.

'That's for you to find out,' the little girl replied, scornfully.

An idea occurred to Lily. 'Did Dimity tell you about Albert?' she asked.

'Of course he did.'

'What does Dimity look like?'

Bella thought about this for a moment. 'He looks very nice,' she said, at last, 'except when he's cross.'

'And does he often get cross?'

'He's cross with you and Nathaniel because you're so slow,' Bella said, and with that she disappeared into the room behind the shop once more.

Mr Popham shook his head. 'She's got such an imagination!' he said.

'Hasn't she?' Lily agreed. Then she said goodbye to Mr Popham and they left the shop.

'So, what do you think?' she asked Nathaniel when they were outside.

'Goodness knows!' Nathaniel said. 'She's a funny little thing, all right. And that business about the buttons was odd. But I think her grandfather's probably right. She's got a lively imagination and that's all there is to it.'

Lily remained unconvinced, but they discussed it no further. When they got back home, they found that Sophie had returned from seeing off Miss Pemberton. Lily showed her the puppet and told her about Mr Popham's dilemma. 'I wondered whether we could do anything about it,' she concluded.

Sophie nodded eagerly. 'What a good idea! After all, we should always try to help people who are less well off than we are. I'll talk to Miss Pemberton when she comes back.'

Miss Pemberton did not return until dinner-time. When she did, she looked tired and strained. Over their meal she told them about the friend whose funeral she had attended. 'She and I grew up together,' she said. 'Her parents and mine were good friends. But she was never a very strong person. She had trouble with her chest for many years, and in the end that's what carried her off. It was a very sad affair, but what made it worse was that the family are so anxious about the threat from bodysnatchers they have been forced to take it in turns to stand guard over the grave for the next three nights.'

'How shocking!' Sophie said.

'Yes, indeed,' Miss Pemberton agreed. 'It will be a dreadful ordeal for them. The sooner the villains behind this bodysnatching business are caught, the better for all of us.'

'Miss Pemberton,' Sophie said, 'Lily has been telling me about an old man called Mr Popham who runs a puppet shop not very far from here. He lives above the shop with his granddaughter, a little girl of about six years of age, but now their landlord has doubled their rent and they cannot pay. So they will be turned out onto the street. I wondered whether there was anything we could do to help them.'

Miss Pemberton smiled and shook her head sadly. 'It is a very kind thought, Sophie, but I'm afraid we are not in a position to dispense charity on such a scale. You see, your stepfather spent a great deal of your inheritance – most of it on gambling, I'm sorry to say. What remains is enough to maintain the house and provide a small income for yourself and Lily to live on. But there is none to spare to help poor Mr Popham.'

As she said this, there was a knock on the front door. A few moments later George appeared in the room, looking as though he had encountered a bad smell. 'There's a Mr Tibbs at the door to see Master Nathaniel,' he announced.

'Well, show him into the parlour,' Miss Pemberton told him.

'Begging your pardon, madam,' George replied, 'but I'm not altogether sure he's the kind of visitor that ought to be shown in. He looks to me like a thoroughly disreputable person.'

'Nonsense, George!' Lily said. 'Mr Tibbs is here on business connected with Master Nathaniel. Now show him into the parlour right away and stop being so snooty.'

'Whatever you say, Miss Lily,' George said with a stiff bow. Then he turned and left the room.

'Oh dear!' Miss Pemberton said. 'I think you've upset him, Lily. He'll be sulking for the rest of the day now.'

Lily sighed. 'He just can't get over the fact that he used to be able to order me around and now he can't,' she said.

When they entered the parlour Tibbs was in the process of examining a plate that stood upon the sideboard. He seemed entirely unabashed that they should find him so engaged.

'Staffordshire cream ware, unless I'm very much mistaken,' he said with a knowing wink. 'Worth a few shillings, I shouldn't doubt.' He put the plate down. 'Mr Rosenberg says he's got something for you.'

'What is it?' Nathaniel asked.

Tibbs shook his head. 'I'm just the messenger boy,' he said. 'The guvnor doesn't tell me that sort of thing, unless I need to know. He respects the privacy of his clients, see.'

'I'm very glad to hear it,' Nathaniel said.

'However, if you'd care to come with me to his office now, I think you might find the visit worth your while.'

Nathaniel and Lily wasted no time putting on their coats and following Tibbs out of the door. He led the way without speaking, only whistling tunelessly to himself from time to time. Just as before, the stairs to Milky Melchy's office were crowded with street people of all ages and descriptions. Many of these turned imploring looks towards Tibbs. One woman, who clutched a shabby-looking rag doll under her arm, tried to throw herself at his feet.

'Oh, Mr Tibbs!' she implored him. 'Can't I see Milky Melchy straightaway? I've got seven children as wants feeding.' She held aloft the rag doll. 'See, here's my little Nancy's doll. Please let me see him now, for Nancy's sake.'

Tibbs regarded her sternly. 'Back in line, Mrs Inchpen, back in line!' he ordered. 'Mr Rosenberg sees everyone in their proper order, as you know. But paying clients goes first.'

Reluctantly, Mrs Inchpen got to her feet and shuffled back to reclaim her place in the queue. Tibbs continued on his way.

At the top of the stairs, Lily took his arm. 'That poor woman with the seven children...' she began.

But Tibbs interrupted her. 'All her children are dead,' he said, 'only she cannot accept it. Deluded, that's what she is. And I'll tell you something else. She's never once come up with a useful piece of information. Mr Rosenberg only sees her out of kindness. Too soft he is, if you ask me.'

After this little speech, he knocked at the door, then opened it and stepped into the office. Nathaniel and Lily followed him.

'Master Nathaniel Wolfe and Miss Lily Campion,' Tibbs announced.

Milky Melchy looked up and smiled, and Nathaniel noticed the glint of a gold tooth at the back of his mouth. 'Please sit down,' the delver said. 'Thank you Tibbs, that will do for now.'

Tibbs went out of the office and shut the door behind him.

'I understand you have news for us,' Nathaniel said.

'Yes, indeed,' Milky Melchy agreed. 'As I told you, sometimes these things take a while, and sometimes they are resolved very quickly. In your case it took next to no time, because a lot of people have heard Cedric Melville's story. It turns out he is rather a famous character.'

'Where can we find him?' Nathaniel asked eagerly.

‘I shouldn’t think you’d want to,’ Milky Melchy replied, ‘on account of the fact that he’s been dead for nearly six months.’

Nathaniel and Lily glanced at each other. The same thought had occurred to them both: could Sir Cedric be the ghost?

‘Everyone agrees that Sir Cedric was a proper gentleman,’ Milky Melchy continued. ‘Always behaved respectably. Never did a thing out of place – until he died, that is. Then he went and left all his money to his butler, Albert.’

‘Did you say his name was Albert?’ Lily asked.

‘That’s him.’

‘Bella asked you if you’d found Albert yet,’ she reminded Nathaniel.

Nathaniel nodded. He turned back to Milky Melchy. ‘Where can we get hold of this Albert?’ he asked.

‘I was coming to that,’ Milky Melchy told him. ‘You see, the thing is, the butler didn’t know what to do with all this new-found wealth. He’d spent his life saying yes sir, no sir, three bags full sir, and suddenly he’d got no one to say it to anymore. And no reason to say it, either. So what did he do? Well, he packed in being a butler for a start. Then he commenced drinking. Soon he was drunk all day long, and all night, too. But that wasn’t enough for him. Oh no! He took to the Black Drop.'

'The Black Drop?' repeated Lily with a frown. 'Whatever do you mean?'

'I see Master Nathaniel understands me,' Milky Melchy said.

Nathaniel nodded. 'I've heard of the Black Drop,' he agreed.

'Laudanum, opium, poppy-juice,' Milky Melchy continued. 'Call it what you like – it's bad stuff in any language. Three months after Sir Cedric passed away, Albert was spending all his time and his master's money in a smoking-house down by the river. And that's where you'll find him today, if you'd care to look. So my question to you both is this: do you wish to pursue your enquiries to the next stage?'

Nathaniel and Lily exchanged glances. If they agreed, they would be stepping into a world that was quite different from any they had known before. Life was cheap among the teeming masses of the metropolis, and Nathaniel had spent most of his days pretty near the bottom of the heap. But he knew perfectly well that there was a layer of the city which was darker and more desperate than anything he had ever known. The entrance to that terrifying underworld was to be found in the opium dens that festered down by the docks, like sores upon the body of the city.

He looked at Lily. 'I can do this by myself,' he told her. 'You don't have to come with me.'

'Try to stop me,' she replied, making her voice sound much braver than she felt.

'Very well,' Milky Melchy said. 'Tibbs will call for you tonight at nine o'clock. But remember, I cannot guarantee your safety. You are entering the devil's kitchen. Once you step inside, anything can happen. Understand?'

Nathaniel and Lily both nodded. 'We understand,' Nathaniel said.

7. THE DEVIL'S KITCHEN

Miss Pemberton was utterly horrified. 'You're actually planning to visit an opium den?' she demanded.

'We have to speak to Albert,' Nathaniel pointed out, 'and that's where he spends all his time. What else can we do?'

Miss Pemberton shook her head. 'It seems to me that these supernatural experiences have had a very bad effect upon you, Nathaniel. You have lost all sense of fear. And fear serves a purpose. It prevents us from walking headlong into danger, as you are proposing to do tonight.'

'You're wrong, Miss Pemberton,' Nathaniel said. 'I haven't lost my sense of fear. I'm terrified of what may happen and I don't mind admitting it. But you've only got two options. You can hide from fear or you can face up to it.'

Miss Pemberton sighed. She turned to Lily. 'Very

well, I give up on Nathaniel. If he wants to put his head into the lion's mouth, then that is up to him. But *you* don't have to follow him. You're only a girl.'

Lily gave a rueful smile. 'When I was thirteen years old, Miss Pemberton, I was getting up at five o'clock in the morning, before anyone else in the house was awake, lighting the fires, heating the water, preparing the breakfast things. I was doing the work of an adult. Nobody said to me, you don't have to do that, Lily, you're only a girl.'

Both Miss Pemberton and Sophie opened their mouths to protest, but Lily interrupted them. 'It's all right, Miss Pemberton. You weren't living here then, and if you had been, things might have been different. I realise that. You're not the kind of person to take servants for granted. Same goes for you, Sophie. You had no say in the way things were run. So I'm not blaming either of you. But my point is this: it's a long time since I was a little girl. When I look back, all I can remember is work, work, work. So I feel the same way as Nathaniel when it comes to it. The world is a hard place, but you have to face up to it. That was how we stopped Mr Chesterfield trying to poison Sophie, and that's the only way we'll get to the bottom of the ghost that's haunting Simeon Makepeace.'

There was silence for some time after she had said

this. Then Miss Pemberton nodded. 'As you wish,' she said reluctantly. 'I see that you are both determined to risk your lives in this venture and there is nothing I can do to stop you. But please take the greatest care.'

She made no further attempt to dissuade them, though it was obvious that she was profoundly unhappy about the whole affair. At nine o'clock that evening Tibbs appeared to collect them.

'Well, I'll say this much for you,' he told them, as they climbed into the hansom cab that stood waiting outside, 'you've got plenty of pluck. Mind you, where you're going, you'll need it.'

The fog that night was even worse than usual, and Nathaniel soon gave up looking out of the window. The driver, who had been chosen by Milky Melchy specially for the occasion, took them swiftly through a warren of streets that grew narrower and narrower as they approached the river. The stink of raw sewage grew stronger all the time, and mingled with the chemical reek of the distilleries and the more ancient odour of decay.

Nathaniel remembered some lines from the Bible that his father often used to quote when he returned from one of his extended drinking binges. *Go not in the way of evil men for they eat the bread of wickedness and drink the wine of violence*, he would intone, before collapsing on the bed in a slumber that was not to be broken for the next twelve hours.

Nathaniel had seldom paid much attention to his father's words, but tonight they seemed to resonate in his head like the echo of the horse's hooves on the cobbled streets as they entered Limehouse Docks. Despite his father's warning, he *was* going in the way of evil men, and what was more, he was taking Lily along with him. He could only hope and pray that they would not encounter violence.

At last the cab drew up outside a row of decaying houses. Everything about them suggested neglect. There was not a brick that wasn't crumbling, nor a timber that wasn't rotten. The whole precarious edifice leaned crazily to one side, and it looked as if a sudden gust of wind might be enough to bring it tumbling to the ground.

'Here we are,' Tibbs said with a grin. 'Buckingham Palace it ain't. You two wait in the cab. I'll go and have a word first.'

He got out of the cab and they watched as he walked up to the front door and knocked three times. The ragged curtains at the window twitched and Nathaniel caught a glimpse of a pale face peering out. Then the face withdrew, and a few moments later the front door was opened by a Chinese girl no more than ten years old. Tibbs spoke to her, but she shook her head violently and tried to close the door in his face. But Tibbs was persistent. Working for Milky Melchy had taught him not to take no for an answer. He thrust himself half into the doorway so that the girl was unable to shut him out. Then he spoke again, this time producing some money from his pocket and handing it over. The girl took the money and counted it. Finally, she seemed to agree, and Tibbs returned to the hansom.

'She says you can go in, as long as you don't make trouble.'

Nathaniel and Lily got out of the cab and Tibbs climbed back inside.

'You're not coming in?' Nathaniel asked.

Tibbs shook his head. 'I never get involved in a client's business,' he said. 'Much better that way. Live longer.' He gave Nathaniel a mirthless grin.

Nathaniel and Lily made their way towards the entrance to the opium den. Even from the street, the smell of the drug was unmistakeable. Sweet, sickly and pungent, it seemed to enter into Nathaniel's bloodstream, so that no sooner had he stepped beyond the threshold than he felt his consciousness subtly changing. The world outside had been exchanged for one in which things moved at a slower pace, and everything seemed dream-like. The shadows were more strange and threatening, the stains upon the wall more intricate and bizarre, the faces of those who lay about the floor on mattresses and cushions more twisted and devilish than any Nathaniel had ever seen before. He felt as though he had entered a scene from a painting. Smoke hung everywhere in sheets, or curled in lazy wreaths towards the ceiling. In every part of the room the devotees of opium sprawled, propped up on one elbow, eyes glazed, sucking the poison into their bodies from glowing pipes, like babies drinking their mothers' milk. The only sound was their satisfied breathing and the occasional mumbling of some delirious addict who spoke with friends or enemies long forgotten, perhaps even dead, but now returned through the narcotic power of the drug.

At a table against one wall sat the keeper of the opium den, a very old Chinese man who was busy preparing pipes of opium. His skin was like parchment and his eyes seemed to be full of an ancient sadness. The little girl whispered to him and he turned to Nathaniel and Lily. 'This house is not for you,' he said. 'It is for those who have lost their way.'

'We want to speak to a man called Albert,' Nathaniel said, trying to sound confident.

The keeper did not react at first, and Nathaniel wondered whether he had been understood. But at last the old man spoke once more. 'Albert comes here to hide.'

'To hide from what?' Nathaniel asked.

'From the world, from his friends and from his own thoughts.'

'You must let us speak to him,' Lily said. 'It's very important.'

The keeper raised one eyebrow. 'That is what people always tell me, ever since I come to your country. You *must* do this, you *must* do that. Never please sir, will you kindly. Only must. But the truth is, I must do nothing. And these, my guests, who come here night after night. They also must do nothing, they must think nothing, they must be nothing. Only then are they happy.'

It sounded like nonsense, and yet Nathaniel felt as if he understood. In the world outside, where everyone was busy piling up money and possessions, the old man was a nobody – a penniless foreigner to be despised and disregarded. But within this room he was a person of great importance. Those who came through his door had given up the struggle to succeed. They wanted to put down their burden and forget their troubles. That was what the keeper offered them, and despite the dreadful squalor of the place, Nathaniel could understand its attractions. You had only to pick up the pipe, put it to your lips, and all your cares would drift away with the smoke.

But then he remembered the old man with the ring and the cupboard in the rock. Nathaniel had spent just a few brief moments in that narrow space, but it had been enough.

'Which one is Albert?' he asked, in a tone that was polite but firm.

The old man nodded. 'I see you are not one of those who gives up easily,' he said. Then he spoke to the young girl in his own language and she tugged at Nathaniel's sleeve. 'This way,' she told him.

They picked their way among the bodies as if they were walking through the aftermath of a battle, where the dead lay just as they had fallen. In the far corner of the room two men were sprawled side by side on a single filthy mattress. They could have been any age, for in the opium den there was no such thing as young and old. Addiction had reduced everyone to the same withered state. Nevertheless, one of the pair stood out from every other individual in the room because his jaw was so hideously swollen that he looked like some kind of monster. Lily gasped when she saw him, but Nathaniel was less shocked. He had seen this condition before. It was called phosphorus jaw, and it was common among those who worked too long in the match factories and came into daily contact with the raw red mineral from which the match heads were made. In time his jaw would rot away completely.

The young girl pointed to him. 'Old Phossy,' she said. Then she indicated his companion who, Nathaniel now realised, was wearing what had once been a smartly tailored three-piece suit, unlike the other occupants, who were dressed in little more than rags. 'Albert,' the young girl said.

Nathaniel thanked her. He crouched down beside the prostrate butler. 'My name is Nathaniel Wolfe,' he began. 'I believe that you used to be in the service of Sir Cedric Melville.'

The butler propped himself up on one elbow and stared at Nathaniel as if he had never in his life seen anything so extraordinary.

'Sir Cedric Melville?' he repeated in a hoarse whisper.

'You were his butler, weren't you?' Nathaniel asked.

Albert shook his head. 'He's dead,' he said at last.

'I know he's dead,' Nathaniel continued, 'but I want to ask you a little bit about him, if you don't mind.'

'Buried under six feet of cold, dark earth. I saw him put there myself,' Albert said, much more loudly this time, 'and that's where he should stay.'

'But he won't though, will he?' Nathaniel asked, speaking as gently as he could.

A spasm of pain crossed Albert's face, and for a moment it seemed as if he might begin to weep. But then another thought occurred to him. 'I couldn't find her,' he said. 'I did try, I swear it, but I couldn't find her.'

'Who couldn't you find?' Nathaniel asked.

Albert gripped him by the arm. 'It wasn't fair to ask me,' he protested. 'It wasn't my business. He should have found her himself.'

'Who should he have found?'

But Albert was starting to become angry now, and Nathaniel's question was lost on him. 'He shouldn't have asked me!' he shouted. 'Why should I have to sort it out for him? I spent enough years sorting things out. Yes sir, certainly sir, anything you say sir. I had enough of it. It's time I was left alone. A little bit of peace, that's all I want. But you won't let me have that, will you? You want to take that away from me, don't you?'

'I'm sorry,' Nathaniel said. 'I just want to know...'

But he was interrupted by the man with the swollen jaw whom the little girl had called Old Phossy. While Nathaniel had been crouching over Albert, Old Phossy had been slowly getting to his feet. He was a big man, and despite the poor physical state to which addiction had reduced him, he still looked capable of considerable violence. 'You heard what Albert said!' Old Phossy interjected. 'He wants to be left alone. So sling your hook before I sling it for you!'

'We just want to ask a few questions,' Lily told him, trying to sound as unthreatening as she possibly could.

But her attempt to calm the situation only succeeded in aggravating it further. From somewhere about his person, Old Phossy suddenly produced a very long and wickedly sharp knife. With surprising speed for someone in his condition, he lunged at Nathaniel.

Nathaniel stepped back just in the nick of time, but not before Lily had let out a scream.

'Enough!'

A giant of a man had entered the room, and now he placed himself between Old Phossy and Nathaniel. There were rings in his ears, and tattoos covered every part of his body that was not hidden by his clothes – even his face and his shiny bald head. Beneath his shirt huge muscles bulged, and he looked as if he could have picked Nathaniel up in one hand and snapped him like a twig. Beside him, Old Phossy seemed once more like a decrepit and emaciated old man. He sank to the ground, defeated, while Albert looked on glassily, as if none of this seemed real to him at all.

'You go now!' the tattooed giant ordered Nathaniel and Lily.

'But we only...' Lily began.

The big man raised one eyebrow. 'You want me to throw you out?'

'We're going,' Nathaniel told him.

They picked their way across the room once more. The old man was still in his place at the table preparing pipes of opium. He looked up at them as they went past. 'You see?' he said. 'In here, nobody *must* do anything.' Then he returned to his task.

Thankfully, the cab was still waiting for them outside.

'Find out what you wanted?' Tibbs asked, when they had climbed back inside.

Nathaniel shook his head. 'All we got was a lot more unanswered questions.'

Tibbs shrugged. 'You came out in one piece, though,' he pointed out. 'Say what you like, I call that a result.' And he called out to the driver to take them home.

8. UNLADYLIKE BEHAVIOUR

'Thank God you are both unharmed!' Miss Pemberton said when Nathaniel and Lily returned. 'I have been sitting here wondering whether I would ever see you again.'

'Tell us everything that happened,' Sophie demanded eagerly.

So Nathaniel and Lily described their experience in the opium den.

'Then you found out nothing?' Sophie said when they had finished.

'I wouldn't say that,' Nathaniel replied. 'For one thing, Albert's reaction confirmed our suspicion that Sir Cedric is the ghost.'

'And for another, we know that Albert was supposed to find someone and he couldn't do it,' Lily added.

'I shudder to think of you visiting that sordid

place!' Miss Pemberton said. 'I should never have allowed it.'

'We knew what we were doing,' Nathaniel reminded her. 'Besides, how else could we have learnt anything?'

'There is another way,' Miss Pemberton declared.

'Really? What's that, then?'

'Tomorrow morning I shall call on Mr Hemlock myself and question him about Sir Cedric.'

Nathaniel looked dubious. 'Simeon Makepeace said that Mr Hemlock flatly denied his firm ever had any dealings with Sir Cedric,' he pointed out.

'With the greatest respect,' Miss Pemberton replied, 'Simeon Makepeace does not know whether he is coming or going. He has been so thoroughly rattled by his experiences that he cannot rightly remember anything, and he is so frightened of losing his job that he might not tell us, even if he could. For that reason, I shall find out for myself what Mr Hemlock knows.'

'And if he's not prepared to tell you?' Lily asked.

'Then I shall use my ingenuity,' Miss Pemberton replied. 'Now, I have some letters to write before I go to bed, so I shall retire to my room. I hope you young people will not stay up too late.'

After she had gone, Nathaniel looked at Lily. 'What does she mean by that?' he asked.

Lily shrugged.

'Sophie?'

'I cannot say,' Sophie replied. 'But you should never underestimate Miss Pemberton. Once she has made up her mind to do something, she can be most formidable. She was prepared to stand up to my stepfather when everyone else was terrified of him, if you recall. I think she may have a trick or two up her sleeve.'

After Sophie had announced her decision to go to bed too, Nathaniel and Lily stayed up a little later, talking over the events of the night and trying to make sense of what had happened. But they were weary from their adventures and it was not long before they parted company and retired for the night.

It was the cold that woke Nathaniel. He had no idea how long he had been asleep, but the room that he slept in was as damp and cheerless as the bottom of a well. He sat up in bed, clutching the bedclothes to him and shivering uncontrollably.

The curtains were closed and the room was as black as pitch, but in the corner a pool of mist glowed faintly. As Nathaniel watched, a tendril reached upwards from it, growing taller and thicker all the time. He held his breath and waited. Gradually, the column of mist began to take on human form, until at last it resolved itself into the figure of the old man who had haunted Simeon Makepeace. He stared directly at Nathaniel, then, raising one hand, beckoned with his index finger.

Weak with terror, Nathaniel could feel the power of the ghost's will, drawing him like a magnet draws a needle. But he was determined not to let the old man take control this time. He shook his head and forced himself to speak. 'I'm not going anywhere with you!' he declared. 'You can beckon all you like.'

Anger burned in the old man's eyes and he began to advance across the room towards Nathaniel.

'Don't come near me!' Nathaniel cried. 'Or I won't help you.' It was the only threat he could think of that might have some influence over the ghost.

The old man hesitated.

'So you *do* want my help?' Nathaniel said. 'Then why don't you tell me what you want?'

Slowly, the old man shook his head.

'You can't speak. Is that it?'

The old man nodded.

'Is your name Cedric Melville?'

The old man nodded once more.

'That cell you locked me in – is it yours?'

The old man bowed his head and gave a great sigh that made his whole frame flicker like a candle in a draught.

'You must have done something very bad to have

been punished like that,' Nathaniel observed.

At this remark, all the strength seemed to go out of the old man. With an obvious effort he lifted his head, and the eyes that looked back at Nathaniel were filled with pain.

'I'm sorry, but I need to know,' Nathaniel began.

It was too late. The ghostly form was already beginning to turn back into mist.

'Wait!' Nathaniel called. 'I don't understand what you want me to do.'

The old man held out his hand and Nathaniel saw the ring glinting on his palm.

'You want me to give it to someone – but who?' Nathaniel cried.

His question remained unanswered, for the old man was gone.

The next morning, after breakfast, Miss Pemberton announced that she still intended to visit Mr Hemlock. 'Would you care to come with me, Sophie?' she asked.

Sophie was both surprised and pleased at the request. People did not often ask for her help. She was more likely to be the one asking for assistance. She and Lily were more or less the same age, but Sophie often felt like a child by comparison. Lily was ready to tackle whatever came her way, whereas

Sophie had spent so much of her time sitting around looking ladylike. I'm like a piece of expensive porcelain, too delicate for anything but display, she thought to herself. What she would have liked most of all was to be brave. But if she could not be brave, then she could at least be useful.

'Certainly I'll come,' she said.

'Thank you, Sophie.'

Perhaps Miss Pemberton isn't quite so bold as she appears, Sophie thought, as she got into the cab beside her guardian. But the real reason for Miss Pemberton's request became evident when they were halfway to the solicitor's office.

'Are you feeling quite all right, Sophie?' Miss Pemberton asked, giving her a rather curious look.

'Perfectly, thank you,' Sophie replied.

'I'm very glad to hear it,' Miss Pemberton said. 'Naturally, your welfare is always my first responsibility. However...' She hesitated.

'However what?' Sophie asked.

'Oh, it just occurred to me that if a young person, such as yourself, were to suddenly feel faint in Mr Hemlock's office, then of course Mr Hemlock would be obliged to take her out into the fresh air, and while this was being done, it might be possible for another person, such as myself, to have a look around the office unhindered. But of course, if you're feeling quite well then no such thing could possibly take place.'

Sophie smiled. Perhaps being fragile had its advantages after all. 'Now that you mention it, I am beginning to feel most peculiar,' she said.

'Oh dear!' Miss Pemberton said, unconvincingly.

Shortly afterwards they drew up outside the offices of Mordecai and Hemlock. The room in which Mr Hemlock worked was situated on the ground floor. It presented an altogether different impression of the company from Simeon Makepeace's shabby room on the floor above. There was a cheerful fire burning in the grate, a couple of comfortable-looking leather armchairs drawn up beside it for the convenience of clients, and a large mahogany desk for Mr Hemlock himself, with a variety of certificates and testimonials hanging on the wall behind it. There was also an imposing collection of legal reference books ranged along a shelf against the wall, contributing to the suggestion that this was the office of a learned man, someone you could turn to for advice and trust to look after your personal affairs.

Mr Hemlock himself was a tall man with a high forehead and an aquiline nose that gave his countenance a rather hawk-like appearance. This predatory air was increased by the way his rather small, beady eyes darted back and forth as Sophie and Miss Pemberton were shown into the room. He shook their hands in turn, but his handshake was weak and flabby. It was like holding a dead fish, Sophie decided.

There was a contradiction here. That much was clear to Sophie before she had even sat down. Everything in the room was arranged to make you feel that you were in safe hands; but everything about Mr Hemlock made you feel exactly the opposite. He's a villain posing as a gentleman, she said to herself. This was something she had experience of. Her stepfather had been exactly the same sort of person.

'Now then, Miss Pemberton, how may I help you?' Mr Hemlock said when they were all seated.

'I have come to seek your assistance in drawing up my will,' Miss Pemberton replied.

'Of course. I should be only too happy to oblige.' Mr Hemlock opened a notebook, picked up a pen and dipped it in an inkwell, ready to begin jotting down details.

But Miss Pemberton was in no hurry to begin. 'Your services were recommended to me by an old friend of mine,' she continued, 'a man who is now regrettably deceased, but with whom I believe you had dealings during his lifetime.'

'Is that so?' Mr Hemlock said, raising one eyebrow. 'May I ask his name?'

'Sir Cedric Melville.'

Outwardly, Mr Hemlock gave no sign that Miss Pemberton's reply had surprised him in any way. Clearly, he was a man who was used to concealing his feelings. Nevertheless, the atmosphere in the room had changed perceptibly. Now there was an added alertness in those beady eyes that darted from Miss Pemberton to Sophie and back to Miss Pemberton.

He took us for no more than a couple of silly women when we walked through the door, Sophie thought to herself. Now he is wondering exactly what game we are playing.

'I think you must be mistaken,' Mr Hemlock said after a moment. 'I can't say I've ever had dealings with anyone of that name.' Then he smiled. 'But of course I would still be most happy to act in relation to your will.'

He was like an iceberg, Sophie decided, with just the faintest thaw on the surface, so that to the outside world he appeared to be just what he said he was: a professional man helping his clients negotiate the intricacies of the legal system. But the real Mr Hemlock lay deep beneath the surface, and nothing would ever penetrate to his frozen heart.

He began to ask Miss Pemberton for details of her personal circumstances.

This is where Miss Pemberton needs my help,

Sophie thought to herself. She had never in her life tried to deceive anyone, and she was not certain she could do so convincingly. But you can't live your whole life like a little child, she told herself. She put both hands to her head and let out a slight moan.

Miss Pemberton turned to look at her and her face was a picture of alarm. 'Are you all right, Sophie?' she asked.

'I'm afraid I feel rather unwell,' Sophie replied, in a feeble voice. 'I think I might be going to faint.'

Miss Pemberton sprang to her feet. 'Good heavens! We must take her outside into the fresh air immediately!' she announced. 'Quickly, Mr Hemlock, take her arm!'

Mr Hemlock looked somewhat bemused, but he got to his feet speedily enough and took Sophie's arm, as Miss Pemberton had suggested. With Miss Pemberton supporting her on the other side, Sophie made her way out of the door, staggering slightly as she went.

'Take deep breaths,' Miss Pemberton said, when they were outside. 'That's good! How do you feel now?'

'My legs are a bit wobbly,' Sophie said.

'I will go back and get a chair,' Miss Pemberton said. 'Mr Hemlock, you stay here and keep hold of Sophie. Make sure she doesn't fall. I will be as quick as I can.'

Mr Hemlock opened his mouth to speak, but Miss Pemberton did not wait to hear what he might have to say. She ran back into the office. Once inside, she wasted no time. She opened the drawer of Mr Hemlock's desk, and there was a bunch of keys, just as Simeon Makepeace had described. She picked them up and began systematically trying them in the lock of the filing cabinet behind the desk. There were a great many keys, so she needed luck to be on her side. Fortunately, it was. The fourth key turned in the lock and the door of the cabinet opened. Inside was a bundle of files, and written on the very first one was the name Cedric Melville. Miss Pemberton stuffed the file into her bag, locked the cabinet once more and replaced the keys in the drawer. Then she picked up a chair and left the room.

Mr Hemlock looked as if he was wondering where she had got to when she returned. Together, they helped Sophie to sit down on the chair. Then Miss Pemberton took a little bottle out of her handbag. 'These are smelling salts,' she told Sophie. 'They will help revive you. Just sniff the contents gently, my dear.'

She held the bottle to Sophie's nose. The smell was acrid and chemical and Sophie recoiled with a grimace.

'I think you'll find that will help to clear the brain,'

Miss Pemberton said, 'and when you're feeling well enough to stand, I suggest we return home right away. I regret that we will have to continue our business on another occasion,' she added, turning to Mr Hemlock. 'Perhaps you would be so kind as to summon a cab?'

He gave a small bow, and within a couple of minutes Sophie and Miss Pemberton were sitting in a hansom on their way back to Chudleigh Street.

'I'm sorry about the smelling salts,' Miss Pemberton said with a smile.

'That's all right,' Sophie replied. 'How did I do?'

'Marvellously!'

'Did you find out anything?'

Miss Pemberton took the file from her bag and held it up.

Sophie gasped. 'So Mr Hemlock was lying all the time?'

'Certainly,' Miss Pemberton agreed. 'The question is, why?'

'What do you think he will do when he discovers the file's missing?'

'I cannot say. However, I don't imagine he'll be terribly pleased. Nor will it take him very long to work out who took it.'

Sophie had been buoyed up by the success of their deception, but now, as the implications began to sink in, her mood changed. The fact that they were in a hansom cab on their way home did not necessarily mean that they had got away with it, she realised. 'Do you think we are in any danger?' she asked.

'Perhaps,' Miss Pemberton replied. 'There is something about Mr Hemlock that makes me think he would be prepared to go to any lengths to get his own way. But we shall meet that problem when it arises. Look! We are home now. Let us go and tell the others what we have done.'

'They'll be astonished!' Sophie said with a smile.

She was right about that.

'I can't believe you stole the file from Mr Hemlock's office!' Lily said, when Miss Pemberton described what had happened.

Miss Pemberton looked quite unperturbed. 'I learned, after standing by helplessly while Mr Chesterfield poisoned Sophie's mother, that, in order to defeat evil, it is sometimes necessary to behave in an unladylike fashion,' she declared.

'But stealing…' Lily insisted.

'Mr Hemlock has been concealing important information about Sir Cedric Melville. We have reasonable grounds to assume that Sir Cedric himself wants us to know that information, and we have taken action in furtherance of that course. That is all. We are not seeking to gain personally from what has happened, only to see that the true facts are revealed.'

'Well, I think you did marvellously,' Nathaniel told her. 'Now, let's have a look inside the file and see what it tells us.'

They all sat down at the drawing-room table and Miss Pemberton opened the file. 'There are three separate documents here,' she said. 'The first one is Sir Cedric's will. Then there are some handwritten notes, taken by Mr Hemlock at the time the will was drawn up. Finally, there is a sealed letter addressed to Sir Cedric's daughter and heir.'

'But Milky Melchy said he didn't have any children,' Nathaniel pointed out. 'That's how come he ended up leaving all his money to his butler.'

'It seems there may be more to the story than is commonly known,' Miss Pemberton said. 'Let me just read Mr Hemlock's notes and the details of the will, and I will see what sense can be made of it.'

There was silence for some time as Miss Pemberton studied the documents while the others waited patiently. Sophie picked up a piece of embroidery she had been working on. Nathaniel stared out of the window at an ancient rag collector, scarcely more than an animated bundle of rags himself, wheeling a rickety handcart up the street, followed by a group of laughing children who mimicked his call. Lily studied the dust motes that drifted lazily through the sunbeams that slanted across the room. No wonder there's always so much dusting to do, she thought to herself, thankful that it was no longer her job to clean the house from top to bottom.

Finally, Miss Pemberton sighed and looked up. 'Oh, what a tangled web we weave!' she said.

'What does it say?' Nathaniel asked.

'Well, it seems that Sir Cedric had a secret relationship with his parlour maid, a young woman called Marigold Hinchcliff,' Miss Pemberton explained, 'a relationship that began as a mere fondness for each other's company, but which soon developed a more intimate nature. She was twenty-two years old when it started, and within a matter of months she learned that she was going to bear him a child. Sir Cedric's reaction, I regret to say, was not what one might have hoped for. He denied that the poor girl's condition had anything to do with him and turned her out of the house.'

'What a beast!' Sophie said.

Lily and Nathaniel only nodded. They had seen more of human nature than their friend, and were not surprised to learn that someone in a position of power should choose to abuse it.

'To his small credit,' Miss Pemberton continued,

'he did come to realise how badly he had behaved when he was a good deal older. But by then, of course, it was much too late. He began making enquiries about Marigold, only to discover that she had died in childbirth in a workhouse just half a mile from his house. Ashamed of his earlier behaviour, he devoted the last months of his life to trying to trace the whereabouts of his daughter, but without success. As a result, when he came to make his will, he left a considerable sum to his butler, Albert, with the instruction that he was to continue the search for the missing girl. The rest of his estate – and a very large amount of money it was, too – he earmarked for his daughter.'

'That must be what Albert meant when he said he couldn't find her,' Lily suggested.

'I wonder how hard he really looked,' Nathaniel said.

'How old would Sir Cedric's daughter be by now?' Lily asked.

Miss Pemberton thought about it for a moment. 'Twenty-eight,' she said finally.

'Then we're looking for a woman, not a girl.'

'Yes.'

'What I'd like to know is what happens to the money if she isn't found?' Sophie asked.

'That's an interesting question,' Miss Pemberton

replied. 'If the proper procedures were followed it would revert to the government, but, of course, if nobody knew that it existed in the first place, then it might just possibly find its way into Mr Hemlock's bank account.'

'So that's what he's up to!' Nathaniel exclaimed.

'But we have the evidence to convict him of fraud,' Lily pointed out. 'All we have to do is go to the authorities with this file and he will be arrested immediately.'

Miss Pemberton shook her head. 'I very much doubt whether it would be that easy. Mr Hemlock would insist that he has been actively seeking Sir Cedric's heir. The fact that he has not chosen to tell Simeon Makepeace about it, or us for that matter, proves nothing.'

Sophie frowned. 'You don't think he really has been searching for her, do you?' she asked.

'Probably,' Miss Pemberton said. 'But not so that he can hand over the money.'

'You mean he might try to kill her?'

'Why not? She stands between him a very large sum of money.'

'And so do we,' Nathaniel pointed out. 'We all know too much about Mr Hemlock now.'

Outside, the sun went behind a cloud and the long fingers of sunlight that had reached across the room were suddenly withdrawn, so that they all felt the chill and shivered as though winter had come in an instant.

'What do you think he'll do next?' Sophie asked, in a voice that was little more than a whisper.

They all looked at Nathaniel, wanting him to say something reassuring, something to make them feel braver than they really were. But all he could offer them was the truth.

'He'll come after us, of course,' he said.

9. THE BOGUS CABBIE

'So what are we going to do?' Sophie asked, as the reality of their position sank in.

'I'd like to pay another visit to Bella Popham,' Lily suggested.

'Bella Popham?' Sophie said. 'The little girl in the puppet shop? What on earth has she got to do with it?'

'There's something strange about her,' Lily said. She told Sophie and Miss Pemberton what Bella had said about her friend who couldn't do his buttons up. 'And then the next time we went to the shop,' she added, 'Bella asked whether we had found Albert yet.'

'It could just be coincidence,' Miss Pemberton pointed out.

'That's what I thought the first time,' Nathaniel agreed. 'But it's happened twice now, and that's not so easy to dismiss. I'd like to find out more about this imaginary friend of hers. He knew about Albert. Perhaps he can tell us something about Sir Cedric's daughter.'

'Well, come on then,' Lily said. 'Let's not waste time talking about it.'

They set off for Popham's Puppet Emporium without delay, but when they got there, they found the shop closed.

'Oh no! I hope they haven't gone already,' Nathaniel said.

'The puppets are still in the windows,' Lily pointed out. 'Let's try knocking.'

Mr Popham soon appeared in response to their knocks. He looked a bit gloomy, but cheered up when he saw who it was and quickly unbolted the door.

'Have you found anywhere to go?' Lily asked when they were inside the shop.

Mr Popham shook his head. 'Nowhere that I can afford,' he said. 'But something may yet turn up. Anyway, never mind my problems, how can I help you?'

'We really came to see Bella,' Lily told him.

'We wanted to ask her about Dimity,' Nathaniel explained.

Mr Popham looked surprised. 'Dimity?' he said.

'It's only a game she plays, you know. There is no real Dimity. But you're very welcome to talk to her. She's always pleased when we have visitors.'

He held back the curtain and they made their way into the room behind the shop. It was like stepping into Aladdin's cave. The walls were covered with tapestries and paintings, and everywhere there were ornaments: curious wooden boxes, plaster statues, small bronze sculptures that must have come from India or China, painted masks with grinning faces and, of course, puppets in various stages of assembly.

'I'm afraid the place is rather crowded,' Mr Popham explained. 'I did a lot of travelling in my younger days, and I could never resist bringing back a souvenir.'

In one corner of the room Bella Popham was trying, without much success, to dress a cat in a doll's bonnet. She looked up and gave them a smile that struck Nathaniel as surprisingly knowing for such a young child.

'I wondered when you'd come back,' she said.

Lily and Nathaniel crouched down on the floor beside her and Lily began stroking the cat, which immediately purred loudly. 'Well, here we are,' she said.

'Last time we saw you,' Nathaniel went on, 'you asked us whether we had found Albert yet.'

'Well, have you?' Bella replied.

'Yes, we have, as a matter of fact. But we're curious to find out how you knew about him.'

Bella tied the bonnet in a bow under the cat's chin and leaned back to examine her handiwork. Satisfied, she turned and regarded Nathaniel as if she might be considering whether he would also look good in a bonnet. 'I've already explained about that,' she said. 'Dimity told me.'

'That's what we wanted to talk about,' Nathaniel continued. 'Please don't be frightened by this question, but we were wondering: is Dimity by any chance a ghost?'

Far from being frightened, Bella looked scornful. 'A ghost!' she exclaimed. 'Of course he isn't. Ghosts wear white sheets and float in the air.'

'Not all of them,' Nathaniel told her. 'Some of them look just like ordinary people.'

'Well, it doesn't matter anyway,' Bella insisted, 'because Dimity isn't a ghost.'

'How can you be so certain?' Lily asked.

'Because ghosts are dead people and Dimity isn't dead. He told me so himself.'

She undid the bonnet and took it off the cat. 'It doesn't suit him,' she said. 'His head's too big.' She got up from the floor, and went and sat in a leather armchair. But that didn't satisfy her for very long.

A moment later she proceeded to turn upside down, so that her legs were resting on the back of the chair and her skirt hung down over her head, showing her bloomers.

'Bella!' Mr Popham said. 'For goodness' sake! What will our visitors think of you?'

Reluctantly, Bella righted herself.

Nathaniel decided to have one last try. 'Has Dimity given you any more messages for us?' he enquired.

There was a pause, during which a distant look came over Bella's face, almost as if she were listening to someone. At last she spoke. 'He says he doesn't know everything,' she told them. 'And soon he won't know anything at all. That's what it's like when you're waiting your turn. You forget the things you knew. That's why you two have to hurry up.'

That was as much as they could get out of Bella. After this cryptic announcement, the little girl insisted that Dimity had gone away and she had no idea when he was coming back.

'Does Bella know that you're going to have to leave the shop?' Lily asked, as Mr Popham was showing them out.

'Well, I've tried to explain, of course,' Mr Popham replied, 'but she lives in a world of her own.' He sighed deeply. 'As you have seen, I acquired many curiosities over the years. I call them my treasures. But they are nothing to me, compared to the happiness of my granddaughter. She is my greatest treasure, and somehow or other I must find a way to look after her.'

Nathaniel and Lily nodded, wishing they could think of something helpful to say. Then they bade him good day and left.

Neither of them spoke much on the way back. It had been a disappointing visit, only serving to remind them of how powerless ordinary people were against those with money on their side and the full weight of the law behind them. Perhaps we will be no more successful in helping Simeon Makepeace, Nathaniel thought gloomily to himself, as he stepped through the door of Number 42 Chudleigh Street.

Miss Pemberton was in the drawing room. She got to her feet when they entered and Nathaniel could tell, right away, that something was wrong.

'Where is Sophie?' she demanded, looking from one of them to the other.

Lily frowned. 'She was here with you when we left.'

'But the message…' Miss Pemberton began.

'What message?' Nathaniel asked.

Miss Pemberton stared at him with a horrified look on her face. 'You sent no message, asking her to join you?'

Nathaniel and Lily shook their heads.

Miss Pemberton sat down on the chaise longue and put her head in her hands.

'What is it?' Lily asked gently, sitting down next to Miss Pemberton and putting her arm around the woman's shoulders. 'What's happened?'

Miss Pemberton looked up. 'They've taken her!' she said. 'Oh, dear God! This is all my fault. What will they do to her?'

'Miss Pemberton, you must try to calm yourself,' Lily said. 'Please tell us exactly what has happened.'

Miss Pemberton made a very deliberate attempt to pull herself together. 'I'm sorry,' she said. 'You're quite right. Well, not long after you two went to call on the Pophams, I had to leave the house on an errand. I got back about a quarter of an hour ago, but to my surprise there was no sign of Sophie. Then George informed me that in my absence a hansom cab had arrived. The driver had come to the door with a message supposedly from you two, saying you urgently needed to speak to her.'

'And she believed him?' Nathaniel asked, incredulously.

'Sophie is such a trusting girl,' Miss Pemberton said. 'It would not have occurred to her that the whole thing might be a trick.'

'So she got in the cab and was driven off,' Lily concluded.

'Exactly.' Miss Pemberton shook her head. 'All this is the consequence of my own piece of dishonesty. I persuaded Sophie to join me in that deception and now she has been kidnapped! If anything happens to her, I shall never forgive myself!'

'We'll get her back,' Nathaniel told her. 'I promise you, Miss Pemberton.'

'We know who has taken her,' Lily pointed out, 'and we know what he wants.'

'You're right,' Miss Pemberton said. 'We must bring the will back to Mr Hemlock immediately and beg him to release Sophie without harm.'

'First, I want to speak to George,' Nathaniel said.

'George knows nothing!' Miss Pemberton replied, impatiently.

'No doubt that's true,' Nathaniel agreed. 'But I would like to speak to him all the same. He may have left out some important detail when you talked to him.'

Miss Pemberton shrugged. 'Very well,' she said.

George was summoned and stood uneasily in the middle of the room.

'We want to ask you a few questions about the man who came to the door earlier,' Nathaniel began. 'We'd like you to try to remember everything he said and did.'

'Not much to remember,' George replied. 'He knocked on the door at about three o'clock, said he had a message for Miss Sophie, and I went and fetched her.'

Nathaniel glanced at the grandfather clock that stood against the wall. Its hands stood at twenty-five past three.

'Did he say who the message was from?' Lily asked.

George shook his head. 'He wouldn't tell me anything. Just that he wanted to see Miss Sophie.'

'So why did you tell Miss Pemberton earlier that he said the message was from Lily and me?'

'Cos that's what Miss Sophie herself told me before she went out. Begging your pardon, Master Nathaniel, but didn't she turn up to meet you then?'

'The message wasn't from us, you fathead!' Lily told him.

George blushed bright red. 'That's not fair, Miss Lily!' he said. 'I wasn't to know.'

Lily nodded. 'You're quite right, George,' she said. 'It wasn't fair at all. I'm sorry.'

George only sniffed.

'There's nothing else you can tell us that might be helpful?' Nathaniel went on, a moment later.

George shrugged. 'I couldn't say, Master

Nathaniel. I'm only a fathead, after all.'

Lily sighed. 'You're not a fathead, George! I was all worked up, that's all.'

'Is that everything, Nathaniel?' Miss Pemberton asked.

Nathaniel nodded.

'Thank you for your help, George,' Miss Pemberton said. 'You may go now.'

George began to walk away. Halfway to the door, he stopped and turned back. 'There was one thing,' he said.

'What was it?' Nathaniel asked.

'Well, it's probably not important at all,' George went on. 'Only I couldn't help noticing it. I mean, it's not the kind of thing you see every day.'

'What isn't?'

'His right ear.'

Nathaniel stared at him, his eyes widening as two pieces of a complicated jigsaw began suddenly to come together in his mind.

'Half torn off it was,' George continued. 'Looked like a dog had eaten it. Anyway, I don't suppose it'll help. Just thought I'd mention it. Will that be all?'

Nathaniel nodded. 'Thank you George,' he said. 'You've been very helpful. Very helpful indeed.'

10. SOPHIE'S ORDEAL

While Nathaniel, Lily and Miss Pemberton were questioning George, Sophie was sitting in a hansom cab, staring apprehensively out of the window and wondering what this mysterious summons could possibly mean. She tried to work out where the cab driver was taking her, but she had not been concentrating properly at the beginning of the journey, and by now the streets through which they passed were entirely unfamiliar to her.

The cab driver had told her very little, only that her friends needed to meet her urgently and that he had been sent to take her to them. She had to admit that she didn't like the look of him. That ear of his was horrible. But it wasn't right to hold things like that against people. Anyway, Nathaniel was prepared to have dealings with all sorts of odd people. He didn't let appearances put him off, and neither would she. She was frightened, but she was also a little bit proud. For once, Nathaniel and Lily needed her help. She was determined not to let them down.

The cab passed through a pair of iron gates into a cobbled yard and pulled up outside some sort of warehouse. The driver dismounted and opened the door. Lily got out and looked around her.

'Where are we?' she asked.

'Your friends are inside,' the cab driver said. 'Just come with me.'

'But what is this place?'

'They'll explain everything. Come on, there's no time to lose.'

He opened a heavy steel door and they stepped into a narrow stairwell. Then she followed him hurriedly up two flights of stairs and along a corridor. He finally stopped outside another steel door and drew back a bolt.

It was then that Sophie began to have her doubts. What would Nathaniel and Lily be doing on the other side of a locked door? She turned to the cab driver. 'What exactly...?' But that was as far as she got. A moment later she found herself propelled forwards into the room. The door was shut behind her and she heard the unmistakeable sound of the bolt being driven home once more. She ran back to the door and beat against it with her fists, demanding to be released immediately. But she knew in her heart that it was hopeless, and when no answer came, she crumpled to the floor and wept.

Her tears were from anger as much as anything else. Anger at herself for being so easily taken in. She had wanted so badly to be brave and resourceful like Nathaniel and Lily. Instead, she had been a fool and walked willingly into a trap. Rather than helping her friends, she had given them one more problem to solve.

Well, weeping would not help, that much was certain. She dried her eyes, got to her feet and looked around her. There was not much light, just what came in through a small window high up in the opposite wall, but it was enough to show her a large bare room, no doubt originally designed as a store-room. She noticed a funny smell which she couldn't place. Not a very nice smell. Slightly sickly. What could it be coming from? The room was empty, except for a table in one corner that was covered with a white sheet. But wait! There was something underneath the sheet. Something that looked very much like... Sophie took a step forward. It couldn't be what she imagined.

She moved closer still, then nervously reached out a hand, took hold of a corner of the sheet and lifted it, just enough to glimpse what lay beneath. She was right! She screamed, dropped the sheet and backed away. She had not been imagining things. There was a corpse on the table!

At that moment, she heard the door being unlocked. She turned and saw Mr Hemlock step into the room. Behind him was the man who had brought her here. Mr Hemlock gave her a mirthless smile. 'Well, Miss Sophie, how pleasant to see you again,' he began, 'though I must admit, you don't look your best, if you don't mind my saying so. I do hope you're not going to have another of your fainting fits.'

'Why have you brought me here?' Sophie demanded. 'And who is that unfortunate individual on the table?'

'The unfortunate individual on the table is a gentleman by the name of Walter Cole,' Mr Hemlock replied, 'a haberdasher by trade. Oh, don't worry. He met his death from entirely natural causes. Heart attack, I believe.'

'Then what is he doing here?'

'He is contributing to the advancement of medicine.'

Suddenly Sophie understood. 'You're a bodysnatcher!' she exclaimed.

Mr Hemlock shook his head and tutted. 'Such an unpleasant expression,' he remarked. 'I am a gentleman of business. Have you never heard of the law of supply and demand?'

Sophie made no reply.

'I see you are not well versed in economic theory. Never mind. I will simplify it for you. There is a demand for bodies and I supply them. That's all.'

'The bodies you supply belong to grieving families,' Sophie told him, angrily. 'You steal them, and in the process you cause a great deal of suffering to innocent people.'

'Well, now, I rather think that's a case of the pot calling the kettle black,' Mr Hemlock observed. 'You were an accomplice to a neat little theft of documents from my office only yesterday, if you recall. But perhaps your morality only works in one direction?' He raised one eyebrow, waiting for Sophie to reply.

She stared back at Mr Hemlock defiantly, determined not to waste another word on him.

'Nothing to say on that score? Well, you must suit yourself. Your friends will be receiving a note demanding the return of those documents just about now. And you had better pray that they respond promptly and without any tricks. Otherwise, like our friend Walter Cole here, you may be making a contribution to the advancement of medical science.'

With that, he turned and left the room. His accomplice remained for a moment longer, staring menacingly at Sophie, his mouth twisted into a lopsided smile. Then he, too, left the room, and a moment later the bolt was drawn home once more.

In the drawing room of Number 42 Chudleigh Street, Miss Pemberton had made up her mind that it was time to go to the police. Nathaniel, however, was less convinced. He recalled his experience trying to convince an overweight and rather red-faced police sergeant that Mr Chesterfield was planning to kill his daughter. The man had completely refused to take him seriously, as he explained to Miss Pemberton.

'In that case, the only evidence you had was entirely supernatural,' Miss Pemberton argued. 'This is quite a different matter.'

'That's true, but Mr Hemlock is a well-respected lawyer, remember,' Nathaniel pointed out. 'He will deny everything and probably suggest that Sophie has run off of her own accord.'

Miss Pemberton sighed. 'Then what do *you* suggest we do?' she demanded.

Nathaniel had no ready answer, but he was saved from having to admit as much by a knock at the front door.

'It is Mr Hemlock himself, come to negotiate with us,' Miss Pemberton said.

Nathaniel shook his head. 'More like one of his henchmen.' He ran out into the hallway. George was already on his way to open the door but Nathaniel stopped him. 'You can leave this to me,' he said.

But when he opened the door, he found that he was already too late. Whoever had knocked was gone. He stepped outside and glanced quickly in both directions. There was no one in the street except an elderly lady walking a small dog. Disappointed, he went back inside. Only when he had shut the front door did he notice the envelope lying on the doormat. He picked it up and examined it. It was addressed to Miss Pemberton and Associates. He brought it in and handed it over.

'Whoever delivered it didn't hang around to make conversation,' he told them.

With trembling hands, Miss Pemberton tore the letter open. Then she read its contents aloud. ' "Return the will by nightfall. Do not contact the authorities. Do not try any tricks. Should you fail to carry out these instructions, you will never see your young friend alive again." '

11. MILKY MELCHY MAKES AN EXCEPTION

'We must do as he tells us,' Miss Pemberton declared. 'I shall take the will to the offices of Mordecai and Hemlock myself at once.'

However, at that very moment there was another knock at the front door. 'Who can it be this time?' Lily asked.

Nathaniel went to the front door once more and opened it to find a tall, pale figure dressed in a fur coat and hat.

'Mr Rosenberg!' he cried. 'Do come in.'

'You look surprised to see me,' Milky Melchy said as he stepped inside. 'You've heard, no doubt, that I do not often set forth from my office during daylight hours. And it's true. Generally speaking, I prefer to let Tibbs carry my messages to clients. But I have news of the gravest kind, Master Wolfe, so grave that I have come in person to tell you.'

‘Then you must come into the drawing room,’ Nathaniel told him. ‘The others are there, though I doubt whether your news is as grave as what has already happened today. Would you like to take your coat off, first?’

Milky Melchy shook his head. ‘I’ll keep it on, if you don’t mind,’ he said. ‘I feel the cold most dreadfully.’

‘As you wish.’

Nathaniel led the way into the drawing room, where he introduced Milky Melchy to Miss Pemberton. ‘Miss Pemberton knows all about our business,’ he explained.

‘I’m pleased to make your acquaintance, Mr Rosenberg,’ Miss Pemberton said. ‘I’ve heard a great deal about you. However, I was just on the point of leaving when you knocked and I’m afraid that my business is most urgent. So I must hurry away.’

‘Of course, madam,’ Milky Melchy replied. ‘I wouldn’t want to hold you up. However, may I be so bold as to ask whether this urgent business you refer to has anything to do with Sir Cedric Melville?’

Miss Pemberton hesitated. Then she nodded. ‘It may do. Why do you ask?’

‘Only because I would advise you in the strongest possible terms to wait until you have heard what I have to say before you continue. My news may have some bearing on how you will wish to proceed.'

'Very well,' Miss Pemberton replied. 'You'd better say what you've come to tell us. But please make haste.'

Milky Melchy nodded. 'As you know,' he began, 'I am in the business of acquiring information. Well, this morning an informant came to see me with the news that the body of a man had been washed up on the shores of the Thames, not far from Lambeth Bridge. His hands had been tied behind his back and his pockets were full of stones.'

'How dreadful!' Miss Pemberton said.

'Dreadful indeed, Miss Pemberton,' Milky Melchy continued. 'But the worst is yet to come, for the drowned man was later identified as none other than Albert Shakestaff, formerly butler to Sir Cedric Melville.' He looked at each of them in turn, finally settling on Nathaniel. 'I think, Master Wolfe, there is rather more to your little enquiry than you have explained to me so far, particularly as I received this note in the post this morning.'

He took a letter out of his pocket and held it aloft to show them. 'It's an anonymous letter, short but not sweet, warning me that unless I wish to meet the same fate as our friend Albert, I should have nothing further to do with anyone making enquiries about Sir Cedric Melville.' He put the letter back in his pocket. 'Now, I make it a general rule not to get personally involved in a case,' he continued, 'on account of the fact that it's bad for business. But this time I'm prepared to make an exception, because I do not take kindly to being threatened. So perhaps you'd like to tell me just exactly what all this is about – the whole story, I mean, not just the parts of it you've been prepared to share with me so far.'

Nathaniel nodded. 'Very well,' he said. 'Let's sit down, and I will tell you as much as I know myself, though I suspect that it's far from the whole story.'

He began with the visit of Simeon Makepeace and then described his own experience of seeing the ghost. He even included his visits with Lily to Popham's Puppet Emporium. 'Though whether that's got any real bearing on the case, I wouldn't like to say,' he added.

When he came to describe the part Miss Pemberton had played in acquiring Sir Cedric Melville's file he noticed that Miss Pemberton had turned bright red. Milky Melchy, however, did not even raise an eyebrow. No doubt he had gone to much greater lengths to acquire information. Finally, Nathaniel told him about Sophie's disappearance and the letter that they had only just received.

Milky Melchy listened carefully without interrupting. 'Do I take it that Miss Pemberton was on her way to return Sir Cedric's will when I arrived?' he asked when Nathaniel had reached the end of his tale.

'That is correct,' Miss Pemberton informed him, getting to her feet.

'Then I strongly advise you to do nothing of the kind.'

Miss Pemberton stared back at him in astonishment. 'Mr Rosenberg, have you completely taken leave of your senses?' she said angrily. 'Miss Sophie's life is at stake.'

Milky Melchy looked entirely unperturbed at this outburst. 'That is precisely why I suggest you do nothing, madam,' he replied. 'Miss Sophie is safe just as long as we are in possession of Sir Cedric's will, because Mr Hemlock believes we will trade it for her safe return. But once he has the will back, he'll want to get rid of any witnesses to this whole affair. Consider the kind of people he has working for him – men who trade in human flesh. We could all end up on the shores of the Thames with our pockets full of stones.'

'So what do you suggest we do instead?' Nathaniel asked.

'We need a witness. That much is clear. Otherwise it's just our word against Hemlock's. Albert would have been perfect if we could have persuaded him to talk. He knew much more about this business than he was letting on.'

'That doesn't help us very much,' Nathaniel pointed out. 'Whatever he did know has perished with him.'

Milky Melchy shook his head. 'I'm not so sure about that,' he said. 'You're forgetting about Old Phossy.'

'The man with the swollen jaw?' Lily said. 'What's he got to do with it?'

'According to my informants, Albert was paying him to act as a bodyguard,' Milky Melchy replied.

'Well, he didn't do a very good job,' Nathaniel observed.

'That's true, but what can you expect? He was an opium addict, like Albert himself. Nevertheless, the two of them spent a great deal of time in each other's company, and I reckon Old Phossy knows a thing or two about what's been going on.'

'So how do we talk to him?' Nathaniel asked. 'We can't go back to the opium den. They won't let us in.'

'No point, anyway,' Milky Melchy replied. 'He's not in the opium den. I've already made enquiries. Old Phossy's gone to Jarvey's Island.'

Lily frowned. 'Where's that?' she asked.

But Nathaniel needed no explanation. He had heard of Jarvey's Island, and it was a name that made him shudder. 'It's not a real island,' he told Lily, 'just the name given to a miserable collection of houses built on wooden piles over the River Bermondsey. It's a stinking place, and the river beneath it is no more than an open sewer.'

'Nevertheless, it's a very good place to hide,' Milky Melchy said.

'Why is that?' Lily asked.

'Because the whole of Jarvey's Island is infested with cholera.'

'Cholera!' Miss Pemberton exclaimed. She gave Milky Melchy an appalled look. 'I hope you are not suggesting pursuing Old Phossy into this place.'

Milky Melchy shrugged. 'Old Phossy's not going to come to us,' he pointed out.

'Don't listen to this man!' Miss Pemberton told Nathaniel. 'He will be the death of you! Don't you understand how cholera spreads? It hovers in the air, like a foul and poisonous miasma that creeps from place to place unseen. Where it settles, the population have no hope. They breathe in that blighted air and the disease enters their bodies. Once that has happened, there is no hope left for them. Those who have not already died are as good as dead. It is into such a place and such a condition that he would lead you.'

Milky Melchy shook his head. 'I'm sorry to

disagree with you, madam, but it's just not true. Cholera is a water-borne disease. Dr Henry Snow proved as much only six years ago. Its victims catch it from drinking infected water, or eating food that has come into contact with that water, not from breathing in polluted air.'

'Then we may enter Jarvey's Island safely?' Nathaniel asked.

Milky Melchy made an equivocal face. 'I wouldn't go so far as to say safely,' he replied. 'They reckon that you should not get within sneezing range of those who have got the disease, and that you do best to cover your mouth and nose at all times. That's the advice I've heard. But it's not the air you've got to fear. It's the food and drink and the carriers of the disease themselves.'

'Enough!' Miss Pemberton cried. 'I absolutely forbid you to go, Nathaniel.'

Milky Melchy spread his hands in a gesture of hopelessness. 'Well, of course, you know best, Miss Pemberton.'

'In this case, I believe I do,' she replied firmly.

'So what is *your* suggestion?' Milky went on. 'You prefer to take back the will and see what happens?'

Miss Pemberton remained silent.

'If I went to Jarvey's Island to look for Old Phossy,' Nathaniel asked, 'would you come with me?'

Milky Melchy nodded his head. 'You see this?' he said, clutching the lapel of the thick fur coat he had still not unbuttoned, despite the warmth of the room. 'My grandfather was wearing this coat when he came to England from Russia a hundred years ago. He walked over a hundred miles to reach a seaport before he could begin that journey, and on the way he had to contend with plague, persecution and poverty. But it did not stop him. He had a will of iron and a very strong love of freedom. They tell me that I look just like him. Whether that is true or not, I would like him to be proud of me. So I will go where I choose in this world and I will not let the Creeping Death stop me.'

Nathaniel nodded. 'Then what are we waiting for?' he said.

12. JARVEY'S ISLAND

The driver brought the cab to a halt when they were still half a mile from Jarvey's Island.

'This is as far as I go,' he declared. 'And a lot closer than most folks would take you.'

Milky Melchy offered him twice the fare to carry on, but he was adamant. 'You get too close to Death and you'll find he starts to take a liking to you,' he told them. 'Keep your distance and keep alive, that's my advice.'

So they were forced to continue their journey on foot. It was not very long, however, before the smell in the air informed them that they were drawing near to their destination, and they pulled up their scarves to cover their mouths and noses.

Jarvey's Island was a patch of ground, bounded on three sides by man-made waterways and on the fourth by the River Bermondsey itself. It was criss-crossed by numerous smaller channels in which all manner of filth had been deposited. Here and there, Nathaniel glimpsed the swollen carcass of some animal caught up against one of the rotting timbers. Elsewhere, the water was stained as red as blood by the chemicals poured into it by a nearby leather works. Bubbles of gas rose to the surface, adding their noxious fumes to the smell of damp and decay that hung over the whole area.

At the backs of many of the houses that stood upon the shoreline, wooden galleries had been constructed so that they overhung the foul water. In these ramshackle edifices numerous families lived, two or three to a gallery. Nathaniel recalled seeing a picture in his grandfather's house of Venice. At the time, he had marvelled to see how a whole city had been built upon a network of canals. Now it seemed to him that Jarvey's Island was like a Venice of drains.

The inhabitants hung over the railings of the galleries, watching the world go by cheerlessly and, for the most part, in silence. Their faces clearly showed the effects of living in such a poisoned atmosphere, for their skin was as white as parchment, save for their cheeks, which were feverishly red. Those that Nathaniel and Milky Melchy encountered on the street stared glassily in front of them, showing no interest in their surroundings and walking about as though in a dream. Nathaniel shuddered to look at them.

'These are the healthy ones,' Milky Melchy reminded him. 'The diseased and the dying are all behind closed doors, too weak to do anything but lie in their own filth and wait for the end. Old Phossy must have been very frightened indeed to have taken refuge here.'

'But can anything be worse than this?' Nathaniel asked.

Milky Melchy nodded. 'Many things. My father taught me that there is no end to human misery.'

They came at last to the address where Milky Melchy had been informed that Old Phossy was hiding. The front door of the house was splintered and hung on one hinge as if it had recently been smashed in. Nathaniel and Milky Melchy exchanged glances, then stepped cautiously inside and made their way up a set of rickety steps towards the top of the house.

On the first landing they heard a woman's voice crying out for help, and through an open door they glimpsed her emaciated form lying on a mattress of straw. She was probably no more than twenty years of age, but she looked like an old woman. Nathaniel took a step towards her and Milky Melchy seized him by the arm. 'Don't be a fool!' he said. 'There is nothing you can do for her.'

'Can't I at least bring her some water?' Nathaniel asked.

'It is the water in this place that has made her sick,' Milky Melchy reminded him. 'I know it is hard but you must stay away from her. All you will do by going in there is endanger your own life.'

Nathaniel nodded. But it was hard, to turn his back on such suffering.

'One day, perhaps,' Milky Melchy told him, 'disease and poverty will be swept away from London.'

'Do you really think so?' Nathaniel asked.

His companion nodded. 'It is what I like to believe.'

By now they had reached the second-floor landing, where they discovered another broken door. 'This is the room in which Old Phossy was supposed to be hiding,' Milky Melchy said.

But it was empty except for a few pathetic items of furniture scattered about. Clearly a scuffle of some kind had taken place.

'If you're looking for Old Phossy, you're too late.'

Their informant was an old woman dressed in a long black shawl. She stood in the doorway, regarding them curiously.

'What do you mean?'

'A couple of big fellows came and took him away

about an hour ago,' she continued. 'Course, he didn't want to go, but he didn't have much choice about it. Broke down the door, threatened to carve him up there and then if he didn't go quietly.'

'Did one of them have half his ear missing, by any chance?' Nathaniel asked.

'Yes, he did. An ugly-looking brute, he was.'

'Come on,' Milky said, 'we're wasting our time here.' He took a coin out of his pocket and dropped it into the woman's open palm. Then the two of them turned back the way they had come.

13. MR MORDECAI

While Nathaniel and Milky Melchy were on their grim errand to Jarvey's Island, Lily and Miss Pemberton continued to discuss their situation at length. Miss Pemberton was far from happy at leaving Sophie's fate in the hands of others. 'It is my fault that this misfortune has befallen her,' she insisted. 'There must be something I can do to remedy the situation.'

There was a cough and they both looked up to see George standing in the doorway.

'Did you want something, George?' Miss Pemberton asked.

'Begging your pardon, Miss Pemberton,' George began, 'and not pretending to understand half of what is going on, being only a fathead, after all.'

'I've already said I'm sorry about that, George,' Lily said with a sigh. 'We're all very emotional just now, that's all.'

'Naturally, Miss Lily,' George continued, 'only it

occurred to me that if you was both to take a slightly less emotional approach to the matter, you might find it more profitable, if you take my meaning.'

Miss Pemberton frowned and shook her head. 'I'm afraid we don't take your meaning at all, George. Can you please be more specific?'

'Well, like I say, I don't claim to know all the ins and outs of the affair,' George went on, 'but all the same, servants hear things, as you know yourself, Miss Lily. And what I hears is that this fellow Hemlock, who it now seems has gone and kidnapped our Miss Sophie, has a partner, a Mr Mordecai. Ain't that so?'

'Yes, George, it is so,' Miss Pemberton agreed.

'And that this here Mr Mordecai used to be a thoroughly respectful sort of gentleman before he took a back seat. Am I right about that also?'

Miss Pemberton nodded. 'Go on, George.'

'Well, why don't you go and see him, then? Tell him what's been going on. If he really is a proper gent, like he's supposed to be, he won't want to have nothing to do with no kidnapping, will he?'

'I do believe you're right!' Lily exclaimed. She turned to Miss Pemberton excitedly. 'What do you think?'

Miss Pemberton nodded. 'I agree. But do we know where he lives?'

Lily thought for a moment. 'Greenwich, I believe. Where exactly, I cannot say, but we could make enquiries at the post office.'

Five minutes later they were seated in a hansom cab on their way to Greenwich, considering what they should say to Mr Mordecai if and when they found him.

'How will we convince him that we are speaking the truth?' Lily asked, 'and not making up some slander upon the good name of his partner?'

Miss Pemberton was silent for a moment. Then she said, 'I will tell you something that I have never told anyone before, Lily. My father was a drunkard.'

Lily did not know what to say. She had always considered Miss Pemberton to be the epitome of respectability.

'I see you are shocked,' Miss Pemberton went on, 'but most families have their secrets. That is mine, and it is not such a great one, really. My father was not a bad man, but he was weak, and alcoholism was the form his weakness took. When I was a child he was a very successful barrister. Gradually, however, his affliction began to affect his career. He was late for meetings, he forgot important details, he insulted clients. By the time I was your age, Lily, he had succeeded in entirely ruining his good name. Of course, he denied it was his own fault and insisted he was simply unlucky or that other people had a grudge against him. But on his deathbed he admitted the truth. His last words to me were these: *a good reputation is a difficult thing to acquire but a very easy thing to lose.*'

Miss Pemberton sighed and stared out of the window of the carriage. 'We must appeal to Mr Mordecai's reputation,' she said. 'Even if he does not believe one word that we tell him, I'm sure he will not wish to see his good name brought into disrepute.'

After some time, they drew up outside the main post office in Greenwich. Miss Pemberton got out and made enquiries. She returned a few minutes later, and gave directions to the cab driver.

Mr Mordecai's house was a large white stucco building on the outskirts of the village. It was imposing enough, yet an air of neglect hung over the garden, as if the owner had ceased to care about its upkeep. Weeds grew among the flowerbeds and hedges were untrimmed. Upon ringing the bell, they were admitted by an elderly butler who showed them into the parlour. Here, too, they experienced the same sense of fading grandeur. The room looked shabby and uncared for. Lily ran her finger along the mantelpiece and tutted at the dust. 'It is not only Mr Mordecai's professional life that he is neglecting,' she observed. 'The servants here are taking advantage of him.'

Just then Mr Mordecai himself appeared. He had once been a big man, that much was clear. But now he was bent over, his cheeks were sunken and there were deep shadows under his eyes.

'I gather you wish to see me,' he said.

'Mr Mordecai, I will not beat about the bush,' Miss Pemberton began. 'I have come to inform you that you are a party, by association, to a number of grave crimes, including fraud, kidnapping and murder. I believe that until this afternoon you have been ignorant of this fact. However, now that you have been appraised of the truth, I have no doubt that you will want to do everything in your power to remedy the situation.'

Such a speech might reasonably have been expected to produce a powerful reaction in most people to whom it was addressed. But Mr Mordecai did not even raise an eyebrow. 'I haven't the least idea what you are talking about, madam,' he replied wearily, 'but if you have come here on legal business, then I suggest you contact my partner, Mr Hemlock, at the offices of my firm. The butler will give you the address.'

'It is about Mr Hemlock that we have come to speak,' Miss Pemberton told him. 'I beg you, please listen to what I have to say.'

Mr Mordecai sighed. 'Very well. If I must.' He sat down. 'But make it as brief as you can.'

Miss Pemberton described Simeon Makepeace's visit to Nathaniel, the appearance of the ghost, her own actions in obtaining the will from Mr Hemlock's office, and the disappearance of Sophie. Mr Mordecai listened to her story without interrupting.

'Sir Cedric's will is in a locked drawer in my study at this moment,' Miss Pemberton concluded. 'If you will accompany me home, I will show it to you myself.'

Mr Mordecai shook his head. 'That will not be necessary,' he said. 'Your story, madam, strikes me as nothing more than the febrile imaginings of a hysterical female. I suggest that you go home and return to your needlework, or whatever it is that you were doing before all this nonsense entered your head. Now, if you don't mind, I have a great deal to be getting on with.'

Miss Pemberton gave him a steely look. 'Have you no concern for your reputation, sir?' she demanded.

'None whatsoever, madam,' he replied. 'I am quite beyond such cares, I can assure you. The world can do me no more harm.'

'Then I must bid you good day,' Miss Pemberton concluded.

'Wait!' Lily said.

They both looked at her in surprise.

'You were once very much in love with your wife, weren't you, Mr Mordecai?' she said.

Mr Mordecai's whole demeanour seemed to change. He stood up straight, and when he spoke, his voice betrayed real emotion for the first time. 'I fail to see what my wife has to do with any of this,' he declared, angrily.

'I think she has a great deal to do with it,' Lily said. 'When she was snatched away, you lost a part of yourself. Anyone can see that. Your house, your garden, your very appearance all testify to it.'

Mr Mordecai stared back at her in silence, but Lily could see that her guess had hit home.

'I think she was a good woman,' Lily continued, 'and I think you miss her very much. Since she left, you have lost interest in everything. But does it not occur to you that she may be looking down on you right now? The dead do not leave us, you know. They watch over those they loved. Even if you have ceased to care about your reputation, Mr Mordecai, I don't believe your wife has. At this moment, I think she may be wondering what has happened to the man she married. She would not expect to hear you speak to Miss Pemberton as you did just a moment ago. She would expect you to be fair-minded and to behave like a gentleman. Don't you agree, Mr Mordecai?'

Mr Mordecai took a deep breath. When he spoke, it was clear that he was making an enormous effort to control his voice. 'Very well,' he said. 'Tell me what you want me to do.'

14. HANGING BY A THREAD

Sophie sat in a corner of the room hugging her knees, as far away from the dead body on the table as possible. She had never been so frightened in her life. She kept expecting the corpse to stir, even though she knew that such a thing was completely impossible. She imagined it sitting up, getting down from the table and walking towards her, stiff-legged, with arms outstretched to throttle her.

'For heaven's sake, pull yourself together,' she told herself. 'A dead body cannot come back to life!' But could she be entirely sure? Once upon a time she would have said that there were no such things as ghosts, but Nathaniel and Lily had shown her otherwise.

She wondered what they were doing now. They must know that she had been kidnapped. What would their next move be? She thought about Mr

Hemlock's threat – if he did not get Sir Cedric's will back by nightfall, she would meet the same fate as the man on the table. But if the will was returned, then Nathaniel and Lily's quest would have failed and it would be her fault.

Why did I not think before getting in the cab, she asked herself. I have ruined everything. But moaning was no good. It was not how Nathaniel would behave. She wondered what he would do. Of course! He would try to escape.

Sophie gazed around the room and considered the possibilities. The one obvious avenue open to her was the window, but that was very narrow and too high for her to reach. Unless she dragged the table across the room and stood on it. But that would mean moving the corpse. She couldn't!

'You *must* do it,' she told herself. Somehow or other she had to summon up the courage.

Reluctantly, she got to her feet and walked over to the table. She stood there for a few moments, trying to force herself to act. What if he is angry with me for disturbing his rest, she asked herself. What if he wants to take me with him, to share his misery? That was what Cedric Melville had wanted to do to Nathaniel. Perhaps the ghost of this man – Walter Cole, that was his name – perhaps the ghost of Walter Cole was hovering somewhere nearby, watching her every move. Sophie looked over both shoulders, but there was no one there.

All this was just putting off the inevitable. Biting her lip, she reached forward and drew back the sheet.

Walter Cole was younger than she had expected, in his thirties perhaps, and dressed in his Sunday best. He lay on his back, eyes open, a faint expression of surprise on his face, as if he had not expected death to come upon him at so young an age. His skin was waxy and almost yellow, his cheeks sunken and his lips completely bloodless. Now that Sophie was this close, the smell of decay was even stronger. She turned and retched.

Afterwards, she wiped her face with a handkerchief. It's not his fault, she told herself. The poor man should be lying in his grave, not stuck here on a table so that Mr Hemlock can sell him to the highest bidder. Then she straightened up and approached the table once more. Now came the worst part of all. She would have to move him!

She slid her hands underneath his armpits. Even through the clothes in which it was dressed, the body of Walter Cole felt dreadfully cold.

'I'm sorry about this,' she told him. Then she began trying to drag him off the table. But it was much harder than she had expected. Death had stiffened the corpse, and she found that she could scarcely move it at all. Bracing herself against the legs of the table, she took a deep breath and tried once more.

The body began to move. Slowly at first, but then more easily. At the same time, Lily began to lose her balance. With a shriek, she tumbled backwards onto the floor, the dead man on top of her.

Pinioned under the weight of that cold flesh, Sophie was almost overcome with horror. She wanted to scream with all the force of her lungs, but somehow she made herself remain calm. Then, with difficulty, she struggled out from underneath the body.

She gazed down at the dead man on the floor. Even if the ghost of Walter Cole had not been angry with her before, he must surely be now. But his face still wore the same expression of mild surprise. It came to Sophie then that he had been a good man when he was alive. She was not sure how she knew it, but she felt quite certain it was true and that he would not want to harm her. She heaved a great sigh that almost dissolved into tears.

But this was no time for weeping. Would her captors have been alerted by the noise? She waited anxiously for several minutes but no one opened the door, and at last she decided they must not have heard anything. Now, to drag the table over to the window. Once again, the noise she made was alarming, but no one seemed to notice. Perhaps they had gone out and left her alone in the building?

She got up onto the table and found, to her delight, that the window was not locked. On the other hand, it was very narrow, and she was not sure she could squeeze through without getting stuck. She opened it as wide as it would go and put her head outside. She was three storeys up. Below her, she could see a flat roof. If she could get onto that, she could climb down via the water barrel at the side. But it was too far to jump onto the roof. She needed a rope.

She drew her head back through the window and got down from the table. There must be some way around this, she decided. Of course! She could use the sheet as a rope. There was a pipe running down the outside of the wall from the guttering. She might be able to tie one end of the sheet to that.

She took the sheet and twisted it to make it stronger. Then she got back up on the table and stuck her head out of the window once more. Right away, she saw that tying the sheet to the pipe was going to be much more difficult than she had imagined. She had to lean right out, then try to pass the sheet behind the pipe, just above one of the brackets holding it to the wall, loop it round and tie a knot. It would have been hard enough using a rope, but with a bulky sheet, it was almost impossible. Almost, but not quite.

At last she had done it and she was satisfied that the knot she had tied was strong enough to hold. Now came the really frightening part. She had to wriggle her way backwards out of the window, take hold of the sheet, and climb down onto the flat roof below. Boys' clothes were so much more sensible, she decided, as she struggled to squeeze her skirts and petticoats through the gap. But eventually she was kneeling on the narrow window ledge. Now she had to transfer her weight to the sheet. If it was not strong enough, it would tear, and she would fall onto the roof below, breaking her legs. Or maybe worse. But there was no point in thinking about it. She leaned over towards the pipe, seized the sheet and swung her legs off the window ledge.

She thought her heart would stop beating as she hung suspended against the side of the building, like a spider clinging to a broken web. But the sheet held her weight. Cautiously, Sophie began to descend. Climbing down a sheet in a skirt that reached your ankles was even more difficult than wriggling backwards out of a window, but she managed, somehow. Unfortunately, the sheet was not long enough, and she saw that she would have to drop the last few feet. She counted to three and let go of the rope, landing badly on the roof and turning her ankle.

At first she thought she had broken the bone, but then she found that, though it hurt a great deal, she could still put her weight on it. Now for the next stage! The water barrel was at the other end of the building. She had to make her way across the roof, but that meant passing three windows. She would have to crawl underneath them. As she was thinking this, she heard a noise, and realised that someone was opening the middle window. Had they heard her? She shrank back against the wall, but, to her relief, no head was stuck out.

She made herself count to a hundred to give whoever had opened the window time to get clear. Then she got down on her hands and knees and began edging her way across the roof. As she drew near to the middle window, she heard raised voices. She stopped, certain that one of them was Mr Hemlock's, and listened more carefully.

'I want to know exactly what he found out,' Mr Hemlock was saying.

'I've already told you,' replied a second voice.

'Well, tell me again.'

'He went to the workhouse that took the girl in,

but the woman who was in charge at the time wasn't working there no more,' the second voice continued. 'So he tracked her down and went to see her.'

They must be talking about Albert, Sophie realised. So the second voice had to belong to someone who knew him. The only person she could think of was Old Phossy.

'And what did the woman tell him?' Mr Hemlock demanded.

'That the girl died in childbirth, but her daughter was brought up in the workhouse until she left to go into service when she was thirteen years old. She stayed in service for five years and the workhouse got a cut of her wages every year. But then it stopped when she left to get married.'

'Whom did she marry?' Hemlock demanded.

'A fellow called Popham. That's all the old woman could tell him.'

Popham, Sophie thought to herself. It couldn't just be a coincidence!

But it seemed that she was not the only one for whom the name struck a familiar chord. 'Where have I heard that name before?' Mr Hemlock mused. 'Of course! The shop we need for storing bodies. Well, well, well. I think we had better go and pay a visit to the old puppet-maker.'

Sophie waited to hear no more. She crawled past the window, climbed down onto the water barrel and from there to the ground. Then, ignoring the pain in her ankle, she made her way out of the courtyard and looked around for a cab. She had to warn the Pophams before Mr Hemlock found them.

15. MRS INCHPEN'S INFORMATION

Mr Mordecai stood in the parlour of Number 42 Chudleigh Street studying Sir Cedric Melville's will. Finally, he looked up from his reading and nodded. 'It is as you say,' he conceded. 'I think, therefore, that our next step should be to contact the police.'

'But what about Sophie?' Lily said. 'Mr Hemlock has threatened to kill her if we do that. At least let's wait until the others get back.'

They did not have to wait very long. A moment later there was a knock on the door and George showed Nathaniel and Milky Melchy into the parlour.

'What did you find out?' Lily asked eagerly, once Mr Mordecai had been introduced.

Nathaniel shook his head. 'Nothing,' he said bitterly. 'Hemlock's thugs had got there before us.' He described the empty room with its broken furniture and the testimony of the old woman next door.

'It seems that we have no choice left but to inform the authorities,' Miss Pemberton declared. 'If you will come with me, Mr Mordecai.'

Mr Mordecai nodded. 'Of course, madam.'

At that very moment, the door to the parlour opened and Sophie herself walked in, dirty, bedraggled and limping, but safe and sound. Miss Pemberton promptly collapsed in an armchair and burst into tears, Lily threw her arms about her friend and the others crowded around, anxious to hear the details of Sophie's ordeal.

When Miss Pemberton had pulled herself together and the others had all stopped firing questions at her, Sophie told them everything that had happened, as briefly as she could, anxious that they should waste no more time. She described the conversation she had overheard through the open window. 'So you see, we must not delay a moment longer. Mr Hemlock and his men are already on their way.'

'I will not hear of you leaving the house again, Sophie!' Miss Pemberton declared.

'But the Pophams…' Sophie protested.

'Lily and I will go and warn them,' Nathaniel said.

'I'll come with you,' Milky Melchy added. 'And perhaps you wouldn't mind staying here, Mr Mordecai, just in case Mr Hemlock sends any of his errand boys after Miss Sophie.'

'Certainly.'

'Here,' Miss Pemberton said. She handed Nathaniel the file she had taken from Mr Hemlock's drawer. 'You'll need to show the Pophams this. But for heaven's sake take care of it.'

'And please, be as quick as you can!' Sophie begged.

Nathaniel nodded and the three of them left without further delay.

The cab that had brought Sophie back from the warehouse was still waiting outside, the horse contentedly munching hay from a nose bag and the cabbie enjoying a quiet smoke. They climbed on board, gave him directions and he set off once more.

It was not far to the puppet shop, but as they approached their destination, they became aware of a dense cloud of smoke rising into the air.

'Looks like somebody's house is on fire,' Milky Melchy observed.

Nathaniel and Lily said nothing, but the same thought had occurred to both of them: was it the Popham's shop that was burning?

Shortly afterwards, the cab was forced to come to a halt by the crowds filling the street. The people of East London did not get much in the way of free entertainment, so when they learned that a fire was in progress, every man, woman and child in the neighbourhood turned out to feast their eyes on the spectacle.

Seeing that it was pointless to continue in the cab, Nathaniel paid the driver and they dismounted. As they hurried round the corner and turned into the Pophams' road, their worst fears were confirmed. Popham's Puppet Emporium was in flames. A chain of fire-fighters had been formed, passing buckets of water from hand to hand to throw upon the blaze; but such tactics were almost useless, for the fire had taken a furious hold on the building. Flames could be seen dancing at the windows, and even as Nathaniel and his companions stood and watched, tongues of fire began licking at the roof.

Nathaniel rushed towards the inferno, but a burly constable seized him by the arm. 'Now, just where do you think you're going, son?' he demanded.

'There's an old man and a little girl trapped inside,' Nathaniel told him. 'Someone's got to get them out.'

'Don't be daft,' the constable replied. 'If anyone's left inside there, they haven't a hope. All you'll gain by running in there is to get yourself killed.'

'We can't just abandon them!' Nathaniel shouted back.

But the constable was unmoved. 'There's a steam-powered fire engine been sent for,' he said, 'the most advanced piece of machinery in existence. In the meantime, if you really want to help, join the chain.'

Despondently, Nathaniel turned back to find Lily and Milky Melchy in conversation with a shabbily dressed woman clutching a filthy looking rag doll in one hand. Where had he seen her before? Of course! She was the woman who had begged to be allowed to see Milky Melchy before anyone else.

'Are you sure that's what they said?' Milky Melchy was asking her.

'On my little Nancy's life, I swear it's true,' the woman assured him.

'Mrs Inchpen says that the Pophams left the house before the fire,' Lily told Nathaniel.

Nathaniel recalled what Tibbs had said of the woman. Deluded, he had called her. 'How do you know this?' he demanded.

'I seen them as they was leaving,' Mrs Inchpen declared, 'the old man and the little girl. Carrying all their belongings in an old cart with a little cat sitting on the top of it. Then, after they left, the others came, kicked the door in and set fire to the place. Horrible they was. A big fellow with half his ear missing and a tall, thin nasty-looking one what seemed to be in charge.'

Perhaps she was telling the truth, after all.

'I knowed 'em, see?' Mrs Inchpen went on. 'The old man was a proper gent. Generous he was, though he didn't have much to be generous with. He used to give me a penny to run an errand for him, sometimes. Old Mr Popham, that was his name. Clever and all. Always reading books.'

She turned back to Milky Melchy. 'It's true, Mr Rosenberg, I promise you. I know what Mr Tibbs says about me. He thinks I don't have nothing useful to tell you, but I've come up trumps this time, ain't I?'

Milky Melchy gave her a patient smile. 'So it would seem,' he agreed.

'But did they tell you where they were going?' Nathaniel asked, impatient with the woman's ramblings.

'Well, they might have done,' Mrs Inchpen said, a wheedling tone coming into her voice now, 'but a body can't be expected to remember everything without a bit of encouragement, can she? I have got seven children to feed, you know.' She held out the rag doll. 'This belongs to my little Nancy,' she said. 'A darling she is, the apple of her mother's eye. And a mother has a duty to look after her children, which ain't easy in this day and age. You understand that, don't you, Mr Rosenberg?'

Milky Melchy nodded. He put his hand in his

pocket and brought out a handful of coins. A gleam came into Mrs Inchpen's eyes and her hand shot out to take the money. But even more quickly, Milky Melchy closed his fist. 'First, the information, then the payment,' he said. 'Now tell us exactly what the old man said.'

Mrs Inchpen scowled briefly, but then her obliging manner reasserted itself. 'Of course, of course. Information first, payment after, though there's some might say I've given plenty of information already,' she observed.

'Just tell us where they were going,' Milky Melchy said.

'Blackheath. A big house where his daughter, Lucy, is in service.'

'What is the name of the people who own it?' Lily demanded.

Mrs Inchpen frowned. 'Lord and Lady something. What was it? My poor old brain ain't what it used to be. Wait a minute! Belmont. That's it. Lord and Lady Belmont.'

Milky Melchy opened his fist and the woman seized the money, melting away into the crowd almost immediately.

'We must go after them,' Nathaniel said, 'but someone has to tell Miss Pemberton where we are headed.'

'I will go back and tell her,' Milky Melchy volunteered. 'But take care. As you have seen, information is not hard to come by if you are prepared to pay for it, and no doubt Mr Hemlock has his sources just as I do.'

'Then let's hope that we get there before him,' Nathaniel said. He thanked Milky Melchy for his help and they went their separate ways.

16. ALL THE FUN OF THE FAIR

'Shouldn't we go round the back, to the tradesmen's entrance?' Lily asked, as they walked up the long gravel drive towards the imposing regency residence of Lord and Lady Belmont.

Nathaniel shook his head. 'You're still thinking like a servant,' he told her.

'I still feel like a servant when I come to a place like this,' she replied. 'Look at the size of it.'

'Well, I don't,' Nathaniel replied. 'And you shouldn't either. They're just human beings, like the rest of us.'

'Extremely rich human beings,' Lily pointed out.

'You just have to show that you're not frightened of them, that's all.' Nathaniel lifted the door knocker and brought it down with a resounding crash.

A few moments later the door was opened by a butler with a face as long as a horse and the thickest eyebrows Nathaniel had ever seen. He frowned at them as if their very appearance caused him pain.

Nathaniel was undaunted. 'Good afternoon,' he began, trying to remember everything he had learned about acting and sounding like a gentleman. 'We are here to make enquiries about a member of your household, a woman by the name of Lucy Popham.'

The butler shook his head. 'There is nobody by that name here,' he said in a voice like an undertaker's. Then he began to shut the door.

Nathaniel put out his hand to stop him. 'We were told she was working here as a maid,' he continued.

'Then you were told wrong. Good day to you.'

With these words the butler closed the door in their faces.

'I thought you just had to show that you weren't frightened of them,' Lily quipped.

'All right then,' Nathaniel replied, irritably, 'what do *you* suggest we do next?'

'Let's go for a little walk,' Lily replied.

They went back down the front steps and followed a path that led around the side of the house. They had not gone very far before they heard the regular *click click* of a pair of shears.

'Sounds like a gardener,' Lily observed.

Sure enough, they soon came in sight of a youth aged about fifteen or sixteen, in a flat cap, shirtsleeves and braces, trimming the top of a box hedge. He glanced in their direction but did not stop working.

'Leave this to me,' Lily said. She crossed the lawn and spoke to him. He put down his shears, took off his cap and smiled. After a few minutes Lily nodded to him and came back.

'Lucy Popham was working here as a maid until last night,' she told Nathaniel. 'Then, this morning, she suddenly announced she was leaving. She didn't give any notice, or state her reasons for going. Lady Belmont is hopping mad, apparently, and no one in the house is allowed to mention her name.'

Nathaniel was taken aback at her success. 'How did you manage to get all this out of the gardener?' he asked.

An expression came over Lily's face that he had never seen before. It was as if she knew something very obvious that he couldn't see. 'I'm growing up, Nathaniel,' she said. 'You may not be aware of that, but some boys are.'

Nathaniel looked at her in confusion, and felt himself blushing bright red.

But then Lily smiled reassuringly. 'Don't worry. We're still friends,' she told him.

They walked back to the village together in silence. In the distance, on the heath, a fair was in progress. Crowds of people were gathered around brightly coloured wagons and stalls, but Nathaniel took no notice of them. Head bowed, he was busy turning over in his mind what Lily had just said about growing up. He felt a fool, though he was not sure exactly why.

As he was thinking this he suddenly realised that it had become very cold. Unnaturally cold. Shivering, he looked up. Standing no more than a stone's throw away under the spreading branches of a horse chestnut tree, was the unmistakeable figure of Cedric Melville.

'What do you want this time?' Nathaniel demanded.

Lily looked at him in surprise. 'I don't want anything,' she said. 'What are you talking about?'

But Nathaniel paid her no attention. His eyes were fixed upon the ghostly figure. Until now Sir Cedric Melville had only appeared in the dead of night. Things must be getting very urgent for him to appear in broad daylight. He was gazing at Nathaniel intensely, as if he wanted to make him understand something very important, but his image was pale and almost transparent in comparison with his surroundings, and it was clearly an effort for him to make himself seen.

'What is it?' Nathaniel repeated, but even as he spoke, the old man's form began to drift apart and in a moment he had vanished.

Nathaniel walked over to where the ghost had stood.

'Was it Sir Cedric?' Lily asked, coming over to join him.

Nathaniel nodded. 'He wanted to tell me something. But what?'

'Look!' Lily was pointing eagerly at a poster tied to the tree by which the ghost had been standing. It was advertising the fair, and there was a long list of attractions and sideshows guaranteed to amaze and delight the public. Like an afterthought at the bottom was written *Popham's Performing Puppets*.

'I reckon that's what he was trying to tell you,' Lily said.

Immediately, the two of them set off across the heath and soon found themselves in the company of crowds of like-minded pleasure-seekers, many of them dressed in their best clothes. It wasn't long before they reached the outskirts of the fair, where musicians, ballad singers and jugglers vied for the attention of the public. Outside brightly coloured canvas tents, showmen stood on wooden boxes and called out invitations to the public to witness the unbelievable contortions of the India-Rubber Man; to look upon the savagery of the Wild Man of the Woods, brought up by wolves in the remote forests of

Hungary; to marvel at the terrifying feats of sword-swallowers, knife-throwers and fire-eaters; or to step inside and have their fortunes told with cards or a crystal ball.

For those members of the public who were not satisfied with just being spectators, there were plenty of opportunities to take part. You could test your skill by throwing hoops or balls at a target; measure your strength on a machine that rang a bell when struck hard enough; and in a roped-off area, anyone who fancied himself as a boxer could try his luck against Alexander the Great, Champion of the Fairground.

The kaleidoscope of sights and sounds was almost overwhelming, and over it all hung the mouth-watering smell of food, for there was every kind of sweet and savoury dish on sale. On the edge of the fair a whole ox was being roasted over an enormous fire while onlookers toasted each other's health with mugs of foaming ale.

'I think all of London south of the river must be here,' Nathaniel said with a grin.

'But where are the Pophams?' Lily asked. 'I can't see any sign of them.'

However, no sooner had she said these words than she felt someone tugging at her skirt, and looking down, found herself face to face with Bella.

'Have you come to see our puppet show?' Bella

asked, looking solemnly up at her.

'We've come to talk to your mother,' Lily told her. 'Is she here?'

'Of course she is,' Bella replied. 'Follow me.'

She led them to a smaller tent on the edge of the fair. Inside, they found Mr Popham and a woman in her late twenties with long blonde hair and sparkling blue eyes.

Mr Popham looked delighted to see them. 'Welcome, my friends!' he declared. 'You come at a most auspicious time. This is Lucy, my daughter-in-law, though I will not be able to say that for very much longer, as Lucy has just informed me that she is getting married again.'

'Congratulations!' Nathaniel and Lily both said.

Lucy smiled and thanked them. Then she kissed Mr Popham on the forehead and told him that she would always be his daughter-in-law, whatever happened.

'He's been so good to me,' she explained to Nathaniel and Lily, 'looking after my little Bella for so long. They wouldn't let me keep her at the big house, you see. Servants aren't allowed to have lives of their own, nor children neither. Well, now they can find another maid to work her fingers to the bone, because I'm joining the fair.'

'Is your husband-to-be one of the showmen?' Lily asked.

'He certainly is,' Lucy replied, 'and not just one of the showmen, neither, but the handsomest man in the fair. His name is Alexander.'

'The prize-fighter?' Nathaniel asked.

'That's him,' Lucy admitted. 'I know people think he must be a brute to earn his living punching other people, but he's ever so gentle, really. And he's been very kind to me. I think I must be the luckiest woman in the world.'

'Actually,' Nathaniel said, 'you're even luckier than you think.'

'What do you mean?'

'Well, it's a long story, but it's worth hearing.'

So, while Lucy and her father-in-law listened in amazement, Nathaniel told them everything that had happened since the visit of Simeon Makepeace. Only Bella looked unsurprised.

'Dimity always said we were going to be rich,' she declared.

Her mother and grandfather laughed. But Nathaniel and Lily were less certain of how to react to this announcement. 'Did he tell you anything else?' Nathaniel asked.

Bella cocked her head to one side, as if listening. 'He's here now,' she declared, 'and he says to look out for the flames,' she added very gravely.

'Of course! The fire. I should have told you!' Nathaniel described the blaze they had witnessed in the Pophams' shop.

Mr Popham sighed. 'I was very fond of the old place,' he said. 'We spent many happy years there. Still, at least no one was in the building at the time.'

But Lucy was anxious to hear more about her inheritance. 'Have you by any chance brought the will with you?' she asked.

'Yes, I have,' Nathaniel told her. 'And I've brought something else, as well.' He handed over the envelope addressed to the daughter of Sir Cedric Melville.

Lucy Popham tore it open. 'There's a ring inside,' she said, 'and a letter.' She began to read.

My dearest daughter,

Though I realise that I have long ago forfeited the right to call you by that name, I hope and pray that this letter reaches you some day and that I have a chance to atone for my wickedness to yourself and to your dear mother.

As you have no doubt learned, your mother and I embarked on a relationship which should have ended in marriage. I even went so far as to buy a wedding ring. But I was too weak to face the disapproval of the world. Instead of offering her my hand, I changed my mind and threw her out onto the street.

It was the act of a shallow, spineless, selfish individual, and you have every right to loathe me on account of it. Yet buried deep within me there was a tiny spark of goodness. I believe it was this spark that your mother loved, though after she left, it grew dull and lifeless. Nevertheless, it did not completely die out, and as the years went by, it began to grow in strength until in my final years it kindled into flame once more. I recognised my wickedness and began to search for your mother in earnest. By then, however, it was far too late.

For some time now I have been ill and recently my doctor has informed me that I have only a matter of weeks left in this world. Therefore, I have drawn up my will. The greater part of my estate is yours. What is left I have bequeathed to my butler, Albert, to assist him in the search for you, so that when he finds you he can hand you this ring. I beg you to take it and to believe me when I say that I wish you all the love and happiness in the world.

Your affectionate father,
Cedric Melville

By the time she had finished reading the letter, Lucy was in tears. 'My poor mother,' she said. 'He did treat her shamefully. And yet I think he paid for it in the end.' She held up the ring to show to the others. 'Alexander's been saving up all the money he gets from his fights to buy me a wedding ring,' she told them. 'Now he can stop saving and we can be married just as soon as we like.'

'And you will be rich,' Lily pointed out.

Lucy shook her head. 'I can't take that in,' she said. 'All my life I've been poor. Suddenly everything's changed. It doesn't make sense.'

'You'll get used to it,' Nathaniel assured her.

'Perhaps,' she said, 'and perhaps not. But for now, I must put this letter and Sir Cedric's will somewhere safe.'

Out of a canvas bag at the back of the tent she took a decorated wooden box that Nathaniel recalled seeing on the mantelpiece of the inner room at the puppet shop. She unlocked the box, placed the will and the letter inside, and locked it once more. Then she replaced the box in the bag and hid it at the back of the tent. The key she tucked away in her purse.

'Oh my goodness!' Mr Popham exclaimed, all of a sudden, glancing at his pocket watch.

The others turned to him. 'What is it?' Lucy asked.

'The puppet show!' he exclaimed. 'We are due to perform in five minutes. Will or no will, the show must go on!'

Lucy and Mr Popham began hastily gathering up the puppets and props they needed for the show.

'Are you going to come and watch?' Lucy asked.

'Of course!' Nathaniel and Lily said together.

'Come along, then,' Mr Popham said. 'Our audience awaits.'

He led the way to a striped puppet theatre that had been erected nearby. The audience, most of them small children, were already seated and waiting eagerly for the show to begin. Lily and Nathaniel took their places among them while Bella went round with a hat, collecting a penny from each customer.

Lucy and Mr Popham ducked underneath the canvas, and a few moments later, with the appearance of Mr Punch, the show began. The characters and the stories were all entirely familiar. Apart from Mr Punch, there was his long-suffering wife and baby, a clown, a hangman, the devil and a crocodile that seemed to be obsessed with sausages. The audience joined in enthusiastically, booing Mr Punch when he behaved badly, cheering his wife when she managed to get her own back, and shrieking warnings whenever the crocodile appeared. Nathaniel and Lily thoroughly enjoyed themselves. After the anxieties they had been through recently, such silliness was a welcome relief.

After the show, they were joined by Alexander, Lucy's fiancé. Up close, Lily had to agree with Lucy's judgement that he was the handsomest man in the fair. And he certainly seemed to be in love with Lucy. His eyes never left her, and though he was a big man, when he spoke to her his voice was full of tenderness.

'They make a good couple,' Lily whispered to Nathaniel.

'I suppose they do,' he agreed. Love was not something he knew much about, though ever since Lily's conversation with the young gardener in the grounds of Lord and Lady Belmont's residence, he was beginning to feel that it might not be too long before he, too, began to feel its power.

'Now we will take the puppets back to our tent. Then I believe a celebration of some kind is in order. Perhaps we should all go and see if that ox is roasted,' Mr Popham suggested.

But when they got back a terrible shock awaited them. The contents of the tent had been ransacked, and in the midst of the chaos stood Mr Hemlock and the man with the mutilated ear.

For a moment, they all stood as if frozen, staring at one other without speaking. Then Lucy's eye fell on the box in which she had hidden the will. It was lying, unopened, on the ground. Slight though it was, that movement was enough to tell Hemlock what he needed to know. Quick as a flash, he bent down and seized the box, lifted the canvas at the back of the tent and ducked underneath. Alexander made an attempt to run after him, but the man with the damaged ear blocked the way, and before Alexander could knock him down he drew a knife from his pocket. The two of them circled each other warily.

There was no time to lose. Nathaniel turned and ran out of the entrance to the tent. Then he stood, looking everywhere for some sign of Hemlock. At first he thought he had lost him completely, but then he caught sight of him, making his way hurriedly through the crowds. Immediately, Nathaniel raced after him, calling out at the top of his voice, 'Stop thief!'

People turned to see what was happening, and when Hemlock realised that he was being pursued, he began to run.

I can catch him, Nathaniel thought triumphantly. Hemlock was a middle-aged man who had spent his life seated behind a desk, whereas Nathaniel was young and fit. No matter how hard he tries, he can't out-run me, Nathaniel said to himself. It's just a matter of time.

But then he realised that Hemlock was heading towards the bonfire over which the ox was being roasted, and he remembered Bella's warning to look out for the flames. He's going to burn the evidence, Nathaniel thought to himself, and there's no way that I can catch him before he gets there.

'Somebody stop that man!' Nathaniel cried

desperately. But though people stood and stared, no one made any attempt to apprehend Hemlock as he reached the edge of the bonfire, flung back his arm, and hurled the box into the very heart of the flames.

'No!' Nathaniel yelled.

Hemlock turned to look at him, his gloating face lit up by the blaze.

By the time Nathaniel drew level with him, the box was already on fire, and it would have been quite impossible to seize it from the midst of the inferno.

'No butler, no will, no evidence,' Hemlock said with a smile of pure malice. Then, turning on his heel, he walked calmly away, and there was absolutely nothing Nathaniel could do to stop him.

Miserably, he made his way back to the tent to find Alexander standing guard over the man with the mutilated ear, who was lying on the ground with his hands tied behind his back. Everyone turned eagerly towards Nathaniel.

'Did you get the box?' Lucy asked.

Nathaniel shook his head. 'He threw it on the fire. There's nothing left but ashes.'

They stared back at him in disbelief.

'Then there's no proof?' Lucy said.

'I'm afraid not.'

They stood despondently in silence for some time.

Suddenly Mr Popham began looking all around him urgently.

'What is it?' Lily asked.

'Bella! Where is she?'

'She was here a moment ago!' Lucy declared, her voice edged with panic and her eyes beginning to fill with tears. 'What can have happened to her? If that man…'

But at that very moment Bella herself walked in through the door of the tent. Seeing everyone staring at her with anxious faces, she stopped in her tracks. 'What's the matter?' she demanded.

'We thought something had happened to you,' Lucy told her.

Bella looked quite unmoved by all this concern. 'Well, you thought wrong,' she said. 'I'm perfectly all right.'

Mr Popham sighed with relief. 'Well, my friends,' he said, 'even if the will has been destroyed, we are no worse off than we were this morning. We have the puppets, Lucy has Alexander, and my most precious possession, Bella, is safe.'

'That's true,' Lucy said, hugging her daughter.

But Bella was not interested in being hugged. 'The will hasn't been destroyed, Grandad,' she insisted.

'I'm afraid it has,' he told her gently. 'It was in the

box I gave your mother, and that dreadful man has thrown it on the fire.'

Bella shook herself free of her mother's embrace and picked up one of the puppets that had not been used in the show: a ballet dancer dressed in a leotard and tutu. Unceremoniously she pulled its head off. Then, like a magician producing a rabbit from a hat, she extracted the will and Sir Cedric's letter from inside the puppet's body.

Everyone stared in astonishment.

'How did they get there?' Lucy demanded.

'I put them there while you were doing your act,' Bella replied, looking rather pleased with herself.

'But they were locked in the wooden box,' Lucy protested.

'I took the key from your purse.'

Lucy shook her head in bewilderment.

'Whatever made you do that?' Nathaniel asked.

'Dimity told me to, of course,' Bella replied.

At first nobody said anything. Then Mr Popham began to laugh. A moment later, Alexander joined in, then Nathaniel. Soon everyone in the tent was laughing until the tears ran down their faces.

17. MR MORDECAI'S WATCH

While Nathaniel and Lily had been on their way to Blackheath, Mr Mordecai had insisted on visiting the warehouse where Sophie had been imprisoned. 'If I am to believe that my partner, in addition to fraud, has been guilty of kidnapping, bodysnatching and possibly even murder, I must see the evidence with my own eyes,' he had declared.

'But what if he returns while you are there?' Miss Pemberton asked.

'Then I shall deal with him myself.'

'He is a dangerous man,' pointed out Milky Melchy.

'He was my partner,' Mr Mordecai reminded them. 'He may still listen to me.'

After some discussion it was agreed that Mr Mordecai and Miss Pemberton would go to the warehouse; Milky Melchy would collect his assistant,

Tibbs, and go to the offices of Mordecai and Hemlock, in case Mr Hemlock turned up there; and Sophie would stay at home in bed. George was given instructions to answer the door to no one other than Nathaniel or Lily.

There was a great deal of protest from Sophie at this arrangement, but since her ankle had swollen up so badly that she could no longer put her weight on it, there was really nothing else she could do.

On the way to the warehouse Mr Mordecai told Miss Pemberton a little more about Mr Hemlock.

'He wasn't a bad man when he first joined the firm,' the solicitor insisted, 'but he was always extremely ambitious. He used to get impatient with my way of doing things. I'm a thorough man, Miss Pemberton. I don't believe in cutting corners. I remember Hemlock told me once that I was far too gentlemanly. I took it as a joke at the time but I see now that he was deadly serious.'

'It's a long way from impatience to fraud, bodysnatching and murder,' Miss Pemberton pointed out. 'How did he become so corrupt?'

'I think the turning point came when his uncle died,' Mr Mordecai went on. 'Hemlock had been expecting to inherit a great deal of money, and I've no doubt that he'd built up a great many debts on the basis of that expectation.'

'But his uncle didn't leave him the money?' Miss Pemberton suggested.

'Exactly. He gave the whole lot to a home for retired sailors in Cornwall. Apparently, he used to go there on holiday when he was a child and it made a very great impression on him. Hemlock was absolutely furious. Stomped about the office for weeks, practically foaming at the mouth. After that he turned very sour.'

'I think this must be the place Sophie described,' Miss Pemberton said as the cab pulled up outside a grim-looking industrial building.

'We must proceed with caution,' Mr Mordecai warned. 'Hemlock or his associates may still be hanging about the building. So no talking from now on. We don't want to let them know we're coming.'

Miss Pemberton nodded.

They made their way through the warehouse gates and crossed the cobbled yard. The heavy steel door was unlocked and they stepped inside, finding themselves in an unlit stairwell. As silently as they could, they went up the stairs towards the room in which Sophie had been held.

It was just as she had described. The table was drawn up beneath the open window and the body of poor Walter Cole was lying on the floor where Sophie had been forced to leave it.

'My God!' My Mordecai exclaimed, forgetting his own injunction that they should remain silent. 'It's all true. What kind of a monster have I been working alongside all these years?'

'That's not a very nice way to talk about an old friend.'

They swivelled round to see that Mr Hemlock himself was standing in the doorway with a pistol in his hand.

'Put that gun away and have some sense, man!' Mr Mordecai exclaimed.

But Mr Hemlock merely shook his head. 'And let you hand me over to the authorities? I don't think so.'

'I'll put in a good word for you,' Mr Mordecai promised.

Mr Hemlock gave a grim smile. 'It will take more than a good word to save my neck, thanks to Miss Pemberton here and her friend, Nathaniel Wolfe. No, I'm afraid this is where our partnership comes to an end, Mordecai.'

Suddenly Mr Mordecai lunged towards his ex-partner. At the same time, Mr Hemlock pulled the trigger of the pistol. There was a flash of gunpowder and in the enclosed space the sound of the shot was almost deafening. A look of surprise came over Mr Mordecai's face and he crumpled to the ground.

Hemlock brandished the gun in Miss Pemberton's

direction, and for a moment she was certain he intended to shoot her as well. But then he shook his head. 'I've decided to spare your life,' he said, 'for one reason only. So that you can carry this message to Nathaniel Wolfe. Tell him that he hasn't seen the last of me. And from now on he'd better look over his shoulder when he's out after dark. He won't just have ghosts to think about now, I can promise you. I'll be back and I will have my revenge.'

With these words, he disappeared down the stairs.

Miss Pemberton knelt down on the ground beside Mr Mordecai. To her relief, she saw that he was still alive.

'Are you badly hurt?' she asked.

'I don't think so,' he said, propping himself up on one elbow.

'Don't move!' Miss Pemberton warned.

'I'm all right,' Mr Mordecai assured her, getting shakily to his feet.

'But surely...?' Miss Pemberton began.

Mr Mordecai put his hand inside his jacket, brought out a large gold pocket watch, and showed it to Miss Pemberton. The case had been badly dented. 'I think this must have saved my life,' he said.

'You're a very lucky man, Mr Mordecai,' Miss Pemberton said at last, after the two of them had finished examining the ruined watch.

'It was a birthday present from my wife,' he said quietly, putting it back in his pocket.

'Then it seems that she really is looking down on you.'

Mr Mordecai nodded. 'Lily was right,' he said quietly. 'The dead do not leave us.'

18. DIMITY

A year later, Nathaniel and his grandfather stood outside the little church of St Michael and All Saints in Wapping. Mr Monkton looked older and more drawn than on the night he had sat across the dinner table from Lord and Lady Huntercombe. Despite the optimism of his letter to Nathaniel, it had taken him many months to recover from being shot.

Together, they considered Sir Cedric Melville's gravestone. It was a surprisingly humble memorial for such a wealthy man – a simple slab of granite with the dates of his birth and death and a single sentence written underneath: '*May God forgive him for he could not forgive himself.*'

'He ordered that inscription just a few days before he died,' Nathaniel said. 'That's what the vicar told me.'

'Well, let's hope he's finally at rest,' his grandfather said. 'And now, I think we'd better hurry inside, or we'll be late for the service.'

They made their way through the graveyard and entered the church itself, joining the little group already assembled around the baptismal font. Mr Popham turned and smiled at them. Beside him stood Bella, Lucy and Alexander. In her arms, Lucy was holding a rather cross-looking baby, whom she now passed to the beaming vicar.

This was not Nathaniel's first visit to the church. He and his grandfather had been there ten months earlier at Lucy and Alexander's wedding. It had been a very quiet affair indeed. Apart from himself and his grandfather, Lily, Sophie and Miss Pemberton, there had been only been the Pophams and a handful of people from the fair.

It had not been how Lucy had planned to get married. Since she had become rich, she had wanted to throw an enormous party. But when the police had arrested the bodysnatching gang – with the exception of Mr Hemlock, of course – and the newspapers had learned all the facts of the case, she and Alexander had been besieged with reporters wanting to hear their stories. So their plans for a grand wedding had been whittled away until, in the end, they had practically been married in secret.

The newspaper men had pestered Nathaniel as well, but he was more accustomed to fame, having been in the public eye before. Nevertheless, he soon grew tired of giving interviews and receiving letters from people who believed themselves to be haunted. Most of them were simply attention-seekers, and Nathaniel replied politely enough, explaining that he did not choose to solve mysteries; the mysteries chose him. Besides, he had his grandfather to look after.

'If these people had their way, I would spend my entire life sorting out old family quarrels and searching for missing heirlooms,' he complained.

His grandfather nodded. 'All the same,' he said, 'I have a feeling that it will not be long before one of those letters strikes a chord, and you are off on another of your missions to put right the mistakes of the past.'

One morning, however, he received a letter that was quite different from all the others. The address on the back declared that the sender was a Mrs Lucy Konstantides, and at first Nathaniel completely failed to recognise the name. But when he tore open the envelope, and saw that it was an invitation to a christening, he remembered that Lucy Konstantides had once been Lucy Popham.

Now that same Lucy Konstantides carefully handed over her baby to the vicar, who dipped its head in the font.

'Dimitri Stephanos Cedric Konstantides, I baptise you in the name of the Father and of the Son and of the Holy Ghost,' he intoned.

All eyes were turned on the little baby. All except Nathaniel's. A familiar chill had begun to steal over his body, and he knew that it meant the presence of someone or something from beyond the grave. He turned, and there, at the back of the church, just as he expected, he saw the faint outline of a ghostly figure.

But this time the phantom did not hold out his hand to proffer a ring. Nor was his expression stern and unyielding. On the contrary, he was smiling, and as his eyes met Nathaniel's, he gave a nod of approval, then raised his hand in a brief wave before disappearing once more.

Red-faced and screaming, Dimitri Stephanos Cedric Konstantides was being handed back to his mother when Nathaniel turned once more to the service.

'What a pity Sir Cedric couldn't have been here to see that,' his grandfather whispered.

'Oh, but he was,' Nathaniel replied.

Afterwards, the congregation repaired to the nearby William Wilberforce Memorial Hall for the reception. This was the very same hall in which Nathaniel's father, Cicero, had held weekly séances in which he had pretended to talk to the dead. Nathaniel had not been back since that time, and it felt odd to be coming here as an ordinary member of the public, to celebrate a new life rather than to peer through the shadowy gates of death.

'Have you ever considered a career in the law?' It was Mr Mordecai. Since the disappearance of Mr Hemlock, he had come out of retirement to take up the reins at his old firm once more. He had made sure that Sir Cedric's estate passed to Lucy with as little fuss as possible, and he had been advising her and Alexander on how best to handle their new-found wealth.

Nathaniel shook his head. 'I don't think I'd be much good in an office, or in a court of law if it comes to that,' he said. 'I think I'd like a more active job.'

'What a pity!' Mr Mordecai replied. 'The legal profession would be greatly strengthened by the admission of more people who have seen both sides of life, as you have.'

'I may persuade him yet,' Mr Monkton said.

The two old men began to discuss a number of celebrated trials that had been taking place recently, and Nathaniel drifted away.

He came across Bella Popham, carrying a tray laden with slices of christening cake.

'Would you like some?' she asked.

Nathaniel took a piece and tasted it. 'Delicious!' he exclaimed.

'My mother baked it herself,' Bella replied. 'She's ever such a good cook.'

'I'm sure she is,' Nathaniel agreed. 'By the way,

have you heard from your special friend recently?'

Bella frowned. 'What special friend?' she asked.

Nathaniel smiled teasingly. 'Dimity, of course,' he said.

But Bella only stared at him blankly. 'I don't know who you mean,' she said. Then she moved away and busied herself offering cake to the other guests.

'Master Wolfe, I'm so glad I've found you. I promised my wife I would introduce you.' It was Simeon Makepeace, and beside him stood a very short, rather plump woman who was beaming all over her face.

'Oh, Master Nathaniel Wolfe, I'm so pleased to meet you,' she began. 'I told my Simeon he should go to you at the very start, you know. I said, that Nathaniel Wolfe talks to spirits all the time. He'll sort out your old man and his ring, and you certainly did.' As she spoke, she kept nodding her head so that Nathaniel began to feel quite giddy from watching her. 'It must be wonderful to have such a gift,' she continued. 'Really, I do admire you so much. I know I should be scared out of my very skin at the sight of a spirit, but I suppose it's nothing to a ghost-hunter like yourself. There are so many questions I've been wanting to ask you.'

Nathaniel looked round desperately for a means of escape. Thankfully, he spotted Lily, Sophie and

Miss Pemberton at the other side of the room. Making his excuses to Mrs Makepeace, he headed towards them.

'Nathaniel, you must have some cake,' Miss Pemberton said.

'I've already had some, thanks,' he replied. 'Do you know, I just asked Bella about her imaginary friend, and she seemed to have forgotten all about him. What do you think of that?'

'Well, I suppose it's only natural,' Miss Pemberton replied. 'She's growing up, and children change very quickly at her age.'

'Besides, she's got a real playmate now,' Sophie added. 'Perhaps she doesn't need an imaginary one any more.'

'Or perhaps they were one and the same all the time,' Nathaniel suggested. The idea had only just come to him, but he suddenly saw how it could make sense.

'Whatever do you mean?' Lily asked.

'Remember what Bella said when we asked her if Dimity had any more messages for us,' Nathaniel continued. 'She said he didn't know everything and soon he wouldn't know anything. That's what it's like when you're waiting your turn. You forget everything.'

'I still don't understand,' Sophie protested.

But Lily was nodding her head excitedly. 'Of course!' she cried. 'He wasn't a ghost because he wasn't dead. He hadn't even been born. He was waiting his turn.'

'Exactly!' Nathaniel agreed. 'Dimity was Dimitri all along.'

'But he's only a baby,' Sophie objected. 'How could he have known all those things that Bella told you?'

'He's a baby now,' Nathaniel said. 'Who knows what he was before?'

'But do you really think that people exist in some way before they are even born?' Sophie asked, dubiously.

'Why not?' Nathaniel replied. 'The doctors, scientists and philosophers like to think they know everything there is to know about life and death, but perhaps it's more complicated than they imagine.'

Just then he glanced across the room and noticed that his grandfather was starting to look very tired. 'I think it may be time for us to set off for home,' he said. 'My grandfather is not as strong as he used to be.'

Sure enough, Mr Monkton crossed the room a few moments later and suggested that they make their farewells. Nathaniel said goodbye to Lucy and Alexander, Mr Popham and Bella, and then he and his grandfather made their way out into the street, where a hansom cab was already waiting. Lily, Sophie and Miss Pemberton went with them.

'When will we see you again?' Sophie asked.

'I don't know,' Nathaniel told her. 'But I've a feeling it won't depend entirely on me.'

'The next time the spirit world comes calling, I suppose,' Lily suggested.

'Don't say such things!' Miss Pemberton protested. 'We don't want any more ghosts, Nathaniel, or any more mysteries to be solved.' She had not forgotten Mr Hemlock's parting words, though Nathaniel had seemed quite unperturbed when she reported them. 'It's time you settled down and lived a normal life,' she told him.

Nathaniel smiled. 'I'll try my best, Miss Pemberton, but I can't promise anything.'

He climbed up into the cab beside his grandfather. Then the cabbie flicked his whip, and Nathaniel was on his way home, leaving behind the bustling streets of London with all their promise, all their menace and all their shadowy secrets. Until the next time.

978 1 84616 520 7 £5.99

It's seven o'clock on a cold, London evening and in a grubby theatre down by the docks, Nathaniel Wolfe watches as his father – the greatest medium in London – takes to the stage. Which of the dead will speak through him tonight?

What Nathaniel doesn't know is that his father is meddling with things he does not understand, things he cannot control. Before the night is over a chilling new world will open for Nathaniel, leading him into a mystery that can only be solved from beyond the grave...

A thrilling story of the supernatural set among the winding streets of Victorian London.

978 1 84616 225 1 £5.99

On the island of Tarnagar is an asylum where you can be locked up for dreaming. Dante works in the kitchen and Bea is the privileged daughter of doctors. When their worlds collide, they are forced to confront the extraordinary evil lurking behind Dr Sigmundus, the ruler of their nation.

Dante is on the run, Bea is in prison and Ezekiel is wounded. Things do not look good for the Púca, the tiny band of individuals who refuse to accept the authority of Dr Sigmundus. And they're about to get a whole lot worse.

In the depths of the Odyll a new kind of evil is about to be born. Its name is Gallowglass and its mission is simple. Hunt down and destroy those who will not obey. Only Dante can stop it. To do so he must face a terrible choice and discover the dark secret at the heart of his own family.

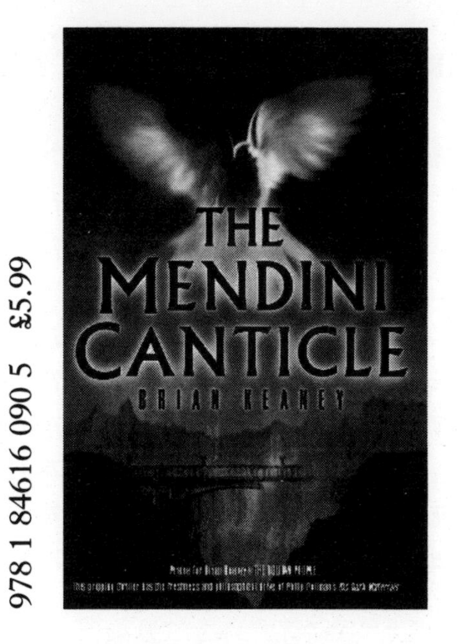

For years Dr Sigmundus has ruled Gehenna with an iron grip. Now he is dead, and the country has a new leader – Dante Cazabon.

As Dante is crowned Sigmundus the Second, a new and terrible phase in the history of Gehenna is about to begin, a phase in which the true meaning of the Mendini Canticle will become horribly clear.

In THE MENDINI CANTICLE, Brian Keaney concludes the thrilling trilogy that began with THE HOLLOW PEOPLE.

OTHER ORCHARD BOOKS YOU MAY ENJOY

The Fire Within	Chris d'Lacey	978 1 84121 533 4
Icefire	Chris d'Lacey	978 1 84362 134 8
Fire Star	Chris d'Lacey	978 1 84362 522 3
The Fire Eternal	Chris d'Lacey	978 1 84616 426 2
The Truth Cookie	Fiona Dunbar	978 1 84362 549 0
Cupid Cakes	Fiona Dunbar	978 1 84362 688 6
Chocolate Wishes	Fiona Dunbar	978 1 84362 689 3
Toonhead	Fiona Dunbar	978 1 84616 238 1
Pink Chameleon	Fiona Dunbar	978 1 84616 230 5
Blue Gene Baby	Fiona Dunbar	978 1 84616 231 2

All priced at £5.99

Orchard Red Apples are available from all good bookshops,
or can be ordered direct from the publisher:
Orchard Books, PO BOX 29, Douglas IM99 1BQ
Credit card orders please telephone 01624 836000
or fax 01624 837033 or visit our website: www.orchardbooks.co.uk
or e-mail: bookshop@enterprise.net for details.

To order please quote title, author and ISBN
and your full name and address.
Cheques and postal orders should be made payable to 'Bookpost plc.'
Postage and packing is FREE within the UK
(overseas customers should add £1.00 per book).

Prices and availability are subject to change.